"This is what you wanted, isn't it, Vincent? To be rid of me."

"Ceara." Vincent sat down on the bed, taking her clenched hands in his. "You're still suffering from shock. You don't mean that."

"On the contrary, I've never felt more clearheaded in my life. You should congratulate yourself—you've gotten your wish. You no longer need to feel burdened by my affections."

He sat back as if she had slapped him. "I beg your pardon?"

"You didn't take what was right before your eyes." Ceara lifted her gaze to meet Vincent's. "Now I'm going to live for me. We'll stay in touch, of course. Maybe you'll come to the city for Christmas."

"By which time you'll have an hour's worth of empty chatter to keep things from getting awkward between us." Vincent leaned forward swiftly, forcing Ceara back against the pillows. "Is that the plan, Ceara?"

"Of course not. I only—"

"Wanted to hurt me as I've hurt you."

Dear Reader,

The holiday season is upon us and what better present to give or receive than a Silhouette Romance novel. And what a wonderful lineup we have in store for you!

Each month in 1992, we're proud to present our WRITTEN IN THE STARS series, which focuses on the hero and his astrological sign. Our December title draws the series to its heavenly conclusion when sexy Sagittarius Bruce Venables meets the woman destined to be his love in Lucy Gordon's *Heaven and Earth*.

This month also continues Stella Bagwell's HEARTLAND HOLIDAYS trilogy. Christmas bells turn to wedding bells for another Gallagher sibling. Join Nicholas and Allison as they find good reason to seek out the mistletoe.

To round out the month we have enchanting, heartwarming love stories from Carla Cassidy, Linda Varner and Moyra Tarling. And, as an extra special treat, we have a tale of passion from Helen R. Myers, with a dark, mysterious hero who will definitely take your breath away.

In the months to come, watch for Silhouette Romance stories by many more of your favorite authors, including Diana Palmer, Annette Broadrick, Elizabeth August and Marie Ferrarella.

The authors and editors at Silhouette Romance love to hear from our readers, and we'd love to hear from *you!*

Happy reading from all of us at Silhouette!

Anne Canadeo
Senior Editor

FORBIDDEN PASSION

Helen R. Myers

Silhouette
R O M A N C E™
Published by Silhouette Books New York
America's Publisher of Contemporary Romance

For Kay Hunter,
with love and thanks for the friendship.
Welcome home.

SILHOUETTE BOOKS
300 E. 42nd St., New York, N.Y. 10017

FORBIDDEN PASSION

ISBN: 0-373-08908-2

First Silhouette Books printing December 1992

Printed in the U.S.A.

HELEN R. MYERS

satisfies her preference for a reclusive life-style by living deep in the Piney Woods of East Texas with her husband, Robert, and—because they were there first—the various species of four-legged and winged creatures that wander throughout their ranch. To write has been her lifelong dream, and to bring a slightly different flavor to each book is an ongoing ambition.

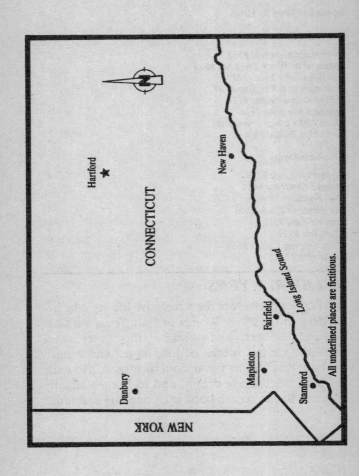

NEW YORK

Danbury

Mapleton

Stamford

Fairfield

CONNECTICUT

Hartford

New Haven

Long Island Sound

All underlined places are fictitious.

Prologue

If it wasn't for Vincent's strong arm around her waist, his astounding tenderness toward her and his barely suppressed fury with the reporters who pressed even closer, Ceara knew she would never have survived her father's funeral, let alone made it to the limousine. As founder and inspiration behind Lowell Publishing, Carson Lowell had been well liked, and it would have been naive of her not to expect the attendance of employees and associates, friends and acquaintances to number in the scores. Her mistake, however, had been in assuming the press would be, if not compassionate, at least discreet. Instead they hovered like vultures descending once the minister concluded the service and she laid a red rose on her father's casket.

"Drive!" Vincent growled to their driver, slamming the car door on the offensive crowd.

Before the limo pulled away from the curb he was drawing her into his arms, offering his broad chest as a pillow; his arms and the all-weather coat he habitually wore like a cape provided additional comfort. Ceara gratefully accepted the sanctuary, the way she had been for the past three days since her father's sudden collapse. Vincent hadn't let her down or stayed politely circumspect the way she had feared he might.

"It's over," he murmured, stroking her hair. "You can cry now."

"I don't want to. You've put up with enough as it is."

"Nonsense. You've been a rock. Carson would have been proud of you . . . and concerned. It's normal and right to grieve, Ceara."

"I'm afraid to admit to myself that he's gone. He was such a strong influence in my life. I feel as though everything is either over or changing."

"Not everything. I'm still here, and I won't leave you unless you send me away."

Reassured, Ceara allowed herself to slide her hand up to his nape while she listened to the vibrant beating of his heart against her cheek; nevertheless, she was cautious about assuming too much. "Do you mean it? I don't want you to keep putting yourself out because of some sense of obligation. You may have been Dad's friend as well as his favorite novelist, but I'd hate for that to be a burden for you."

"The important question is what am I to you?" he asked, quietly.

Why was he asking that when he knew the answer? He *had* to know. Ceara shifted to search his face. "Maybe you should be telling me what you want to be?"

Never had anyone fascinated her as did this dark, charismatic man. For endless seconds time was caught in a breathless place where there was only the subtle shifting of the car as it sped toward Manhattan, and the feel of their hearts beating against each other, stronger than ever before.

"Ceara." Her name was a wistful sigh, made increasingly poignant when he pressed a fervent kiss against her forehead. Then he drew her back against his chest, his embrace more intimate, more promising. "We've much to talk about, you and I."

"I'd like that."

Under the circumstances it seemed almost sacrilegious to feel such a surge of hope and happiness, but she did. If he only knew how much. She had wanted to tell him that she had been waiting for those words, waiting for *him*, for years. How could this be wrong when everything she had ever felt toward Vincent Dante was good and positive?

Ceara wouldn't have minded if the trip to the apartment took longer, but once there she discovered Mrs. Green had stepped out a moment to run to the market. They were still alone. "Shall I check the kitchen and see if there's a pot of tea ready?" she asked after they removed their coats.

"Are you sure you wouldn't like to lie down? I could get it and bring it to you."

"Mrs. Green's been through enough. The last thing she needs is returning to find you in her kitchen," she replied, reminding him of the undeclared cold war between him and their housekeeper. "Besides, I could use a chance to feel useful."

Without giving him time to reply she escaped down the hall. But after seeing the steaming kettle on the stove, she thought of how good some pastry or sandwiches might taste now that her nerves were having an opportunity to unclench their grip on her stomach. She decided to ask Vincent if he would like to join her in a light meal.

When she returned to the living room, however, she found it empty. A sound from her father's study drew her there. Maybe he had decided he needed something stronger than tea or what was offered in the bar. Maybe he wanted the cognac kept on the credenza. It wasn't quite noon, but she couldn't blame him...or could she? she wondered, taking in the scene that greeted her.

Never had she been faced with anything more incriminating. Her father's desk drawers were open; several of his journals lay on the blotter. Oblivious to her presence, Vincent stood reading one, his expression indescribably chilling.

"Though I've never had reason to betray his privacy, if you'd asked, I would have told you precisely where he kept them," she said softly, unable to hide her disappointment or the shiver of trepidation that rushed through her.

To his credit he didn't try to make any empty excuses. "I apologize, but...when I said we needed to talk, I meant it," he replied, his tone grim. "There are things you don't know about me. Things I'd prefer you hear from me rather than reading about them here."

"Obviously. They must be some secrets. How long have you been keeping them from me?" She crossed the room and took hold of the book, felt his resistance and met his black, unreadable eyes with bleak determination. When he relented and let her have it, she glanced down, experiencing a pang as she recognized her father's determined scrawl. *Oh, God, they did it, didn't they? I'm about to discover they both let me down.* She knew it was true as soon as she saw the date.

"November 15, 19—" Startled, she glanced at Vincent. The entry had been written seven years ago. To be precise, on the night of her eighteenth birthday.

" 'This evening I elicited a promise from Vincent,' " she began, her dread exposing itself in the fine trembling of her hands. " 'I felt compelled because of my growing concern over his and Ceara's deepening emotional ties. It's inevitable that one day soon he'll realize fully the...the woman emerging inside the girl, though at the moment I believe they remain safely preoccupied with their remarkable, blossoming friendship. I must believe that.' "

"Ceara, don't do this," Vincent entreated. "Not now of all times. Later when you've rested and feel stronger..."

" 'Was it jealousy that drove me?' " she continued, ignoring him and swallowing the hurt that was beginning to leave a bitter taste in her mouth. " 'In all honesty I can't deny envying their unique rapport. They're two separate and distinct halves that, despite their considerable age difference, create a stunning, single entity whenever they're together. But, God forgive me, she's my child and he—friend though I call him—is too sophisticated, too experienced and too *scarred* for a deeper, lasting relationship with someone of Ceara's special sensitivity.

" 'I'm not proud of what I've done. It's created a chasm between us, subtly altering our friendship. However, I've no doubt he will keep his word and refrain from encouraging a relationship that is beyond...chaste. Vincent is as honorable in maturity as he was reckless in his youth.

" 'Regardless, my responsibility was and is to Ceara. I would do anything to protect her from heartbreak and grief, which I fear is all that could come from giving her heart to a man as haunted by his past and driven by his talent as is Vincent Dante. Nevertheless, the mantle of authority is a heavy one. My only hope is that Ceara never learns of our gentleman's agreement. At least not before she's old enough to understand how it was the right and necessary action for me to take.' "

When Vincent tried to take the book from her, Ceara clutched it to her chest. "No. Tell me what you were going to do—tear out the incriminating pages? Take the entire volume?"

"I hadn't decided yet."

"But you considered it, didn't you?" she challenged, seeing the last seven years of romantic daydreams and fantasies take on a foolish and humiliating cast under the glare of harsh truth.

"I won't deny the idea appealed to me when I considered how it might keep you from looking at me the way you are now."

She shook her head. "How I look can't possibly begin to reflect how I feel. Oh, Vincent—" She bit back a sob. "How could you?"

"I had my reasons, and if you'll sit down, I'll try to explain some of them to you."

Some? Not all? That had her coiling more tightly within herself, and when he tried to lead her to the love seat on the other side of the room, she evaded his touch. "You of all people knew how strongly I fought my father's efforts to protect me from life and treat me like a child."

"To him you *were* a child."

"I was a human being with feelings, a woman's feelings."

"Believe me, I was and am aware of that."

"Why should I believe you? How am I ever supposed to believe you again when you've proved yourself a master at deception and manipulation? A person with true and deep feelings for another wouldn't find it so easy to do what you did."

He didn't blink; he barely seemed to be breathing. "What makes you think it was easy?"

She wouldn't listen. All she could think about was that for seven years, longer, he'd held her at arm's length because of some ridiculous agreement he had made with her father. Did he have any idea how guilty, foolish, *undesirable* she felt?

"I think you'd better leave," she said, bowing her head.

"Don't say that. Don't send me away."

"It appears I have some intensive reading to do, and I'd prefer to do it alone."

"I'll wait in the living room. Undoubtedly you'll be confused and have questions. I can . . ."

"Lie to me, as you've been doing for years? No, thank you."

"Ceara."

Tears began spilling down her cheeks. *"Will you get out!"*

"Amen to that." Mrs. Green appeared in the doorway, looking sturdy and righteous. "You'll leave, Mr. Dante, or I'll phone building security."

Vincent spun around as though he was going to invite her to try. Then he shot Ceara a look, dark with despair and burning with emotions she refused to let herself trust.

She had to turn her back to him or lose the remnant of control that remained. "A promise is a promise, Vincent. Keep yours, and . . . and go away."

Chapter One

He burst through the double doors of the hospital, the black all-weather coat he had flung over his shoulders against the late September wind and rain billowing behind him. Droplets of water clung to his eyelashes, his eyebrows and his hair. No doubt more rain was sluicing off his clothes, creating a veritable stream on the otherwise glistening linoleum floor, but he didn't care. His attention, his entire being was focused on something far more important. Life. A specific life. His mind was tuned to her, his senses were scanning for evidence of her, his entire body leaned forward, as though drawn by a magnetic force.

He had no doubt the image he cut as he strode toward the nurse's station was an intimidating one, a not entirely sane one; he could see as much from the way the two nurses there eyed him, their gazes widening with surprise and more than a trace of anxiety. But rather than feeling contrite, he was aware of his intent, his deliberateness. The darker, dangerous side of his nature was reigning, and that side had come to the conclusion that getting information out of trained sentinels—and these two crones looked as though they had stood guard at Methuselah's sickbed—would be easier after knocking them off balance. If necessary, he would do more than disrupt their comfortable routines; he would bulldoze his way right through them.

"Ceara Lowell," he demanded, still yards away from the station.

Though his voice left no room for evasion let alone argument, the elder of the two women, the one who reminded him of a photo he had once seen of Churchill's bulldog, lifted her chin and gave him a haughty glare that announced he could stop right where he was and answer a few of their questions first. It was the taller, less militant one who extended her bony arm like a wounded egret and pointed to the hallway angling off to the right behind them.

"But that's ICU and there are *no* visitors allowed," the bulldog added, shooting her comrade a look promising such treason would not go unpunished. "Not until the doctors say otherwise."

He didn't bother replying, nor acknowledging the angry "Sir!" she barked when it became clear he was determined to ignore her warning. In fact, both women were vanquished from his mind before he finished circling the booth. There was, however, no denying how much harder his heart was now beating because of this newly gleaned information.

Beneath his turtleneck sweater a trickle of sweat slid down his spine. Intensive Care...Father in Heaven. When the police telephoned explaining they had found his unlisted number in the purse of an accident victim, he had known immediately who they were referring to. A million and one questions had flooded his mind, but all the officer had been able to tell him was that she had been brought to this Stamford, Connecticut, hospital. There had been no information on her condition. During the race down from Mapleton, he had convinced himself it wouldn't be bad. She might have a few scratches and some nasty bruises, but he would get her discharged right away. He'd had to reassure himself of that, otherwise he might easily have driven his own car off the road. Now that he knew how wrong he was he felt as though his feeble hold on the remaining shreds of his sanity was slipping.

It was all his fault. Everything. She had been devastated when he left her apartment yesterday; he didn't need a degree in clinical psychology to determine that. But emotionally incapacitated himself, he had left because he had needed some time alone, a chance to think. Once again selfishness, his stupidity, had caused this. He couldn't be more to blame if he had been steering the damn car himself. His fault. No matter how upset with him she was he should never have left her.

The first room on the left was empty, but he heard something in the one on the right. He paused, and holding his breath, forced himself to look inside, only to discover the occupant was an elderly man. There were so many tubes and wires attached to him that he appeared caught in a man-size spiderweb. Even the nurse checking on the hapless victim looked in a hurry to be done with the task and away from the unhappy scene.

He exhaled to purge the rising tide of emotions boiling within him, then drew another breath. Sharp smells assaulted his senses: disinfectants, medicines . . . scents that accompanied illness and death. As he continued his trek down the hall, they reinforced all the reasons why he didn't like hospitals; and his aversion was nothing compared to Ceara's. She loathed them, and by now could very well be in a state of panic, another reason why he needed to find her. If she had to be here, the least he could do was see to it she didn't spend any more time alone than necessary.

At the third room he came to an abrupt halt and stared into a small cubicle filled with several nurses, doctors and machines. He grew claustrophobic just observing them from the outside. But what filled him with an unspeakable dread was how everyone was hovering around the single bed like hunched-shouldered mourners—and how their patient was lying there so still, he wasn't certain she was breathing.

Ceara. Fear, acute and painful, gripped his heart; another spasm shut off the air flowing through his throat. Ceara. Dear Lord, were they connecting her to those machines or...?

A nurse flipped switches and turned dials, and a screen lit up, something began beeping. Soon the machine beside it was humming. Relief brought an overwhelming weakness, and he clutched the doorjamb to steady himself. He hadn't arrived too late, after all. She was alive; and as long as she was breathing, there was hope.

Like someone caught in a trance, he stepped into the room, only to have his next step blocked. Glancing down, he saw an arm stretched before him, an arm belonging to a nurse. He stared. It was ludicrous for someone of her far less significant size to think she could physically impede him. But at least, he noted belatedly, there was compassion beneath the trepidation in her eyes.

"I—I'm sorry, sir. You can't come in here."

"I must."

Their exchange was quiet; nevertheless, it attracted the attention of one of the men dressed in a seal-blue surgeon's uniform. "Wait a minute, Nan." Though bloodshot, sharp and gauging eyes studied him. "Don't I know... are you related to Miss Lowell?"

"She has no family living. Her father passed away earlier this week. I'm..." He fell silent. Who was he indeed? A man who had known her since she was little more than a child because fate had decreed her father should publish his books? A self-possessed recluse who had felt everything he was and believed in change the moment he looked into her magical brown eyes? A fool who, out of respect for her father, had made a promise he had been paying for dearly ever since? A soulless wretch who knew he would have difficulty finding a reason to remain living if she was no longer part of this world? "I'm Vincent Dante," he said, opting for simplicity, his gaze once again drawn to Ceara. "I'm a family friend."

"Family friends aren't authorized to visit ICU patients, Mr. Dante," the nurse replied, withdrawing her hand but remaining rooted where she was. "You'll have to wait in the visitors' reception area. I assure you, we're taking good care of Ms. Lowell, and we'll let you know the moment—"

Even as Vincent stiffened, preparing to turn on her with the full extent of his wrath, the doctor intervened. "Hold it, Nan. If I'm not mistaken, this is *the* Vincent Dante. You know, the mystery writer?" he added when it became clear she hadn't made the connection.

"Oh? *Oh.*" Her eyes widening, she took a respectful, backward step. "My goodness."

"You'll have to excuse us, Mr. Dante. This has already been a hectic day, and it's far from over." The doctor's tone, though remaining weary, warmed with amusement. He extended his hand. "Phil Bernstein. I admire your work."

Though Vincent went through the obligatory courtesy of a handshake, he didn't take his eyes off Ceara. "How bad is she...?" He couldn't say it. It was hard enough to view the cuts and bruises already marring her flawless skin; the bandages swathing her head all but hid her long ash-brown hair. It filled him with terror, and he was hard-pressed not to rush to her side, take her in his arms and entreat, no, *demand* she open her eyes.

"We don't know yet. Wait," Bernstein replied, raising a hand as Vincent shot him an impatient look. "I can tell you that except for the blow she sustained on her head she didn't receive any other life-threatening injuries in the accident. But that one strike was brutal and, as a result—I'd better amend that to say I think as a result of it—she's slipped into a coma."

"You *think?*"

"It's not uncommon for head trauma patients to be out of it for a while, but even considering the injury, this is a slightly deeper coma than expected. I've come to the conclusion—and mind you I wouldn't want to have to stand before a panel of experts and qualify this—the condition could be emotionally induced."

Vincent had to swallow to keep the panic out of his voice. "I see. And when do you think she'll come out of it?"

"I'm a surgeon, Mr. Dante, not a fortune-teller. Despite the great strides we're making, the medical community is still in the elementary stages of knowledge when it comes to understanding the brain and what part individual willpower plays in the process. There's every reason to believe she'll regain consciousness, but it'll be when she's ready.''

That was something at least.

''The first officer at the accident scene said the accident occurred on a fairly straight section of road,'' Dr. Bernstein continued. ''He didn't see any apparent reason for her to have lost control of her car. But he also said it was obvious she'd been crying. My question to you is whether you feel losing her father would encourage her to hide from the world for a while?''

Feeling the full weight of his forty-four years, Vincent closed his eyes and pinched the bridge of his nose. ''She'd recently learned some upsetting news besides that. Maybe…what I'm trying to say is yesterday we— *I* hurt her. Deeply.'' It was a difficult confession to make, and when Vincent reopened his eyes, he wasn't surprised to find the doctor staring at him with unabashed curiosity. Although he knew there was some truth to the old theory about the benefits of confiding in strangers, it wasn't his way and he instinctively withdrew within himself, merely adding, ''I want to be with her.''

Clearly disappointed at the intriguing but miserly offering, the doctor took a moment to consider the request. Finally he inclined his head. ''I can't see how ten minutes would hurt.''

''You misunderstand. I mean to stay with her.''

''But that's impos—''

''Doctor.'' It was only one word, and almost a whisper, but Vincent had long ago perfected a talent for brevity, and an equally useful one for being profound with a mere glance. He remained silent and still as he watched the shorter man wrestle with the dilemma of how to deal with this new demand.

"Damn you," Bernstein muttered at last, massaging the back of his thick neck. "You tell me you're responsible for jeopardizing the well-being of this young woman and I'm supposed to let you near her without getting a full explanation first?"

"Yes."

For what seemed like an eternity Vincent withstood the doctor's exasperated and wholly perplexed stare, as well as the looks from the others in the room who had heard the outburst and were waiting for the results. Being all too familiar with the way people responded to him, he felt more fatalistic than uncomfortable. He knew all they saw was the shell of who he was: a huge, dark and—as Carson had put it, though he had spoken with more bemusement than sympathy—unapproachably fierce-looking man, who at this moment was behaving with an arrogance in keeping with many people's expectations of his appearance.

So be it, he thought dispassionately. He had no interest in pleasing or appeasing *everyone*. Right now all he cared about was Ceara and convincing this overworked, skeptical physician that he could be trusted.

Something about his unflinching, determined stare must have struck a nerve, because the equally dark-featured man offered what could have been either a grimace or wry smile. "All right. But do I have your word you're here for her benefit and not some belated or ill-founded guilt trip? Because the one thing I am certain of is that she could very well hear whatever you might say to her, and right now I don't want her to have to deal with anything more arduous than opening those pretty brown eyes of hers."

Vincent stiffened again, experiencing a sharp stab of jealousy. "Believe me, Doctor, if I thought it would be in her best interest to stay away, I would leave now." And eventually he might have to, he acknowledged to himself, as he once again considered Ceara's innocent and achingly youthful face. "But I know for the moment, at least, she needs me."

Phil Bernstein shot him a look, indicating the verdict on that wasn't in yet, but he cleared the room with an impressive speed that spoke eloquently of his stature in the hospital. Just before leaving himself, he paused. "Answer me this—is she a fighter?"

Vincent thought of the bright and effervescent young woman who effortlessly attracted people to her with her warmth and charm. "In her own way she's indomitable."

A ghost of a smile lifted the corners of the doctor's naturally down-turned mouth. "Then I hope the first thing she does when she opens her eyes is to punch you cheerfully in that overbearing nose of yours."

Vincent nodded but couldn't summon a smile of his own. "You'll never know how much I agree with you, Doctor."

Finally alone, he experienced a moment of uncertainty and fixated on the suddenly loud machines. He studied each as if he really cared to know what they were and how they operated when the truth was that he didn't give a damn about them as long as they continued to function. What he needed was a moment to compose himself before facing her. After all, this was the one person who now had firsthand experience at understanding how human, how *flawed* he really was.

At last he approached the side of her bed and brushed the backs of his fingers across the top of her hand. Such exquisite softness. All it had taken was one accidental touch years ago, the innocence of fingers reaching for the same fallen scarf, and ever since he had been susceptible to any excuse to touch her.

How vulnerable she looked; the insignificant outline of her slight frame beneath the white bed linens only emphasized it. What a contradiction to the spirit and energy with which she normally approached life. It tore at his heart to think of all she had been through this past month. Would she ever forgive him for adding to her pain?

As Carson had accurately said of his daughter, Ceara thrived best in an environment where there was a high level of enthusiasm and activity. His own interests centered around his preference for isolation, a preoccupation with drama and the darker sides of life, and his inescapable pessimism. Once he had recognized his multileveled attraction to her and the unique and mysterious chemistry between them, he should have done whatever necessary not to explore it. At the least he should have taken steps discouraging her from getting overly caught up in him. But, no, he, who had long denied himself the pleasure of letting anyone get too close, care too much, had been seduced by the fantasy of having a living, breathing angel adore him. He was fully guilty of encouraging a dangerous game of hearts.

Carson had seen it and had been terrified by its power. Little did his friend know he had actually been relieved when a promise had been demanded from him. Like an addict, he had discovered that not since he was a boy did he possess less willpower to resist temptation.

Seven years...for seven years he and Carson had kept their secret, and he, his word. But what a toll it had demanded, *was* demanding.

Those wonderful inquisitive eyes were closed, locking him out. Her velvet-brown lashes had never looked starker against her pale face. Vincent leaned closer and traced the fine line of a winged eyebrow and then stroked his fingers down her cheek, along her jaw, tracing the delicate contours of her small oval face. It was a luxury, an intimacy he would never have risked at any other time. Yet it was one he would have gladly sacrificed for her consciousness.

What had she been doing driving around here? he wondered. Had she been coming to see him? To say she had forgiven him? He dared to hope, but knew in the end all that mattered was for her to awaken.

"Don't do this to me," he whispered. "Don't you know if you gave up, my life would be over, as well?"

She remained as quiet as death, in a place impossible for him to reach. All he could do was wait and reassure himself with the theory that as long as he could see her, she wasn't completely lost to him.

Phil Bernstein stopped by at the end of his shift. After examining Ceara, he lingered, leaning against the bed's footboard. Dressed in a white coat, which ordinarily would have provided an attractive contrast to his brown hair and olive complexion, it now served only to emphasize his own weariness and his glassy eyes.

"Still determined, I see," he said, breaking the silence that lingered heavily in the room.

At first Vincent's impulse was to ignore him. Hours ago he had drawn a chair beside Ceara's bed, so he could hold her hand while meditating, and he had seen no reason to stop during the examination, though he accepted, even applauded the doctor's conscientiousness. This intrusion on the silence, however, was unwelcome. "Don't you have a home to go to?" he muttered.

"Mmm...but an empty one at the moment. My wife is visiting her parents in upstate New York, and I hate the way the house sounds when she's not in it."

Vincent preferred living alone, having convinced himself life was a less painful ordeal that way; nevertheless, Bernstein's words touched an empathetic chord in him. It allowed him to offer in return, "Ceara's often accused me of having an inimitable stubborn streak. There's no reason to disappoint her after all these years."

"'All?' How long have you known each other?"

He hesitated, then decided to let the man think what he would. "Eight. She was seventeen the first time her father invited me to their New York apartment."

"Is she going to be happy to see you when she opens her eyes?"

"Right now all I care about is that she does open them."

"Admirable, but it might be prudent to have a few lines prepared. Silence can grow damn uncomfortable after 'welcome back.'"

Vincent twisted his lips into a mirthless smile. "You're fishing, Doctor, and with no bait on your hook."

"Is that what my problem is? What kind would you prefer I use?"

With a sigh Vincent released Ceara's hand and shifted to consider the man watching him. "Now don't tell me, let me guess...you moonlight as a psychiatrist in your free time?"

"You wouldn't say that if you saw my grades in the subject from school," Bernstein replied with a self-deprecating laugh. "No, as I said, you're one of my favorite writers. The fact damn little gets into the press about you makes you all the more of a curiosity to me."

Vincent could understand that easily enough. His publishers received a great deal of mail inquiring about him, as well as constant requests from the media for interviews, all of which he chose not to deal with. "Speaking of the press," he said, determined to control the direction of their conversation, "I'm surprised no one has contacted the newspapers yet. Grateful, of course, but surprised. Ceara's somewhat well-known in her own right. As you've no doubt figured out her father was—"

"Carson Lowell, founder and chief swami of Lowell Publishing. I figured it out. That's where I saw your picture. It was in the morning paper. You escorted her to the funeral. You had a beard and you wore your hair longer, otherwise I would have recognized you sooner."

Yes, he had looked less than . . . civilized because he had just finished a book when news came of Carson's death. Dropping everything, he had rushed to Ceara's side without taking time to get presentable. This morning when he saw the picture himself, he'd immediately ordered his man, Townsend, to go for his shears.

"When I'm working, I tend to immerse myself totally in the project at hand," Vincent said, aware he owed the doctor a token something in gratitude for making his stay possible.

"I'd consider growing a beard myself if it didn't get so hot under all those masks and hats we wear in the operating rooms. I'll bet you find one helps deter salesmen who come to the front door?"

"The day anyone gets past the fence and front gates without an invitation is the day I hire a new security service."

"And how do they work against young women with major crushes?"

Vincent narrowed his eyes. "I thought I heard you warning your staff not to speak arbitrarily when they came in here because you were concerned with what your patient might pick up?"

Though Bernstein had the grace to look sheepish, he replied, "It's common knowledge we doctors rarely follow our own dictums. In any case, I apologize." When Vincent failed to respond, he rubbed his whisker-stubbled jaw and straightened. "I guess I'd better leave while I'm ahead. If you're interested, there's a couch in the ICU family waiting room where you can stretch out."

"I'm not leaving her."

Phil Bernstein glanced from Vincent to Ceara. "Well, if willpower counts for anything, I wager I'm leaving her in good hands."

Willpower had to count, Vincent thought, moments after the doctor said good-night and left. It just had to.

Bourne lit a match and touched the flickering flame to the folder he'd just dropped into the wastebasket, then took Anna in his arms. "Now do you believe it's over?"

For another moment she continued to watch the flames spread until they engulfed the incriminating documents. Finally she buried her face against his shoulder. "You'll leave soon, won't you?" she said, tears slipping free and soaking his shirt. "You'll go back to that bloody island you're so crazy about and forget me."

Suppressing a sigh, Bourne lifted her head and kissed her. "You know I must. My life is there. And yours is here," he added before she could protest. "Go now. The police will drive you home. No doubt someone's already there waiting for you."

"Matthew will never give me what I've had with you," she cried.

"Lovely Anna . . . you might discover it could be better. All you have to do is give it a chance." With a last, surprisingly greedy kiss Bourne placed her at arm's length. "Be happy, darling."

He waited until the police car had driven off before he collected his own leather jacket and exited the building. Outside he found the sun shining and across the street in the park he spotted the first flowers of spring. He decided he would take a walk before he caught his own ride to the airport. It would be a perfect way to say goodbye to Boston . . . and Anna.

Vincent closed the paperback copy of his fourth novel, which he had found at the hospital's coffee shop early this morning. He had been reading it off and on to Ceara because she often said it remained one of her favorites.

"Good old Bourne," he murmured, running his thumb over the glossy black-and-silver foil cover of the book. "No wonder you were fond of him. He was the one protagonist I'd almost allowed to let his heart get in the way of his head."

With a sigh Vincent put the book on the table beside the bed, sat back in the chair and dragged his hands over his whisker-stubbled face. Fatigue was beginning to get the best of him. He had been here for over twenty-four hours and had yet to allow himself a moment of sleep. His eyes burned and were gritty, his head felt ready to burst and his throat was a raw ache. And all for naught since there was still no change in Ceara's condition.

He leaned forward, rested his elbows on his knees and pressed his clasped hands to his lips. "Open your eyes," he rasped. "Do it. Now. You know you want to. There's nothing to be afraid of, not any longer. I'll never reject you again. That part of the past is done with. We can start over. Somehow. Ceara... for the love of God. *Please.*"

Unable to bear it for a moment longer, he pushed himself to his feet and strode across the room. *Calm down,* he ordered himself, raking his fingers through his already hand-mangled hair. If he couldn't get himself back under control, he would have to leave, get an hour of sleep and come back later. Ceara wouldn't benefit from his losing control, and Bernstein wouldn't stand for it. He could use the time to wash up, too. Ceara didn't need to regain consciousness and find some wild man hovering over her.

Behind him he heard a rustle. Not altogether certain his mind wasn't playing tricks on him, he spun around. Yes, it had been his imagination; she looked as peaceful as when he first entered the room yesterday.

Then the machines started to register something happening.

He hurried to her side. Leaning over her, he touched her hand, her cheek, and whispered her name. To his amazement her lashes fluttered in reaction.

"Yes!" His heart soared. He had the strongest urge to laugh. "Do it. Open your eyes."

Slowly she did, her eyelids working as though they were an impossible burden to budge. They lifted slightly...fell shut...opened again, and looked around.

The first emotion he saw reflected in their depths was complete confusion. Then Vincent saw them darken with fear. He sought and grasped her hand. "Don't be afraid. You're all right, and I won't leave you."

For the first time she focused on him. "Vincent."

"Yes, my...yes, it's me."

Fire and ice replaced the fear, and even before his heart could do more than lurch painfully in his chest, Ceara weakly dragged her hand from his grasp.

"What—what are you doing here? I told you...I never wanted to see you again."

Chapter Two

She closed her eyes because it was easier. At least that way she didn't have to see the room, deal with the knowledge of where she was...and she could avoid the shock and hurt mirrored in his eyes. No matter how he felt, it couldn't be any worse than her own pain or humiliation.

But Ceara soon realized that even behind her closed lids it was impossible to escape Vincent. She had known him too long; his image was burned into every one of her brain cells. She supposed she would have to die to escape him, and therein lay the ultimate irony, since she had almost died, hadn't she? Why else was she here?

Vincent. From the first time her father had mentioned him he had intrigued her. A mystery writer, her father had explained, adding he was an odd character—but then what writer wasn't? A man with a good mind, he had continued, going on to describe him as mysterious and charismatic, retiring yet sincere and possibly the most melancholy soul he had ever met. Hindsight allowed her to see her father hadn't been immune to Vincent Dante's powerful magnetism, either. Or perhaps he had simply seen in him the younger brother he never had. Whatever the case, when she met Vincent, she had recognized something else that would prove as devastating as it was undeniable: she would never lose her heart to anyone as quickly and completely as she had to him.

Ceara opened her eyes slightly and peered at him from beneath the protection of her lashes. As expected, it hurt—in her heart and in her head. Angry and bitter though she was over what he had done, seeing the state he was in, his uncombed coal-black hair and his haunted, bewhiskered face, made her ache for him.

However long she had been lying there, he had been keeping vigil by her side; there was no reason to doubt that. It would be his way. Dependable, solicitous Vincent—but only to a point. And now she understood why those limits existed.

She tried to remain indifferent as she studied his profile, a stark silhouette dominated by a strong brow, aquiline nose and square, cleft chin. That, too, proved impossible. She could be blinded in the next instant, and she would forever carry in her memory the image of those slashing black eyebrows running low over obsidian eyes, eyes more than one interviewer had described as hypnotic. Fatigue had turned them bloodshot, deepened the lines at their corners, the shadows beneath, but it did nothing to dilute his power. He was staring off into space, and Ceara could only wonder at the inner storm he viewed. No, she decided, more than likely he was contemplating the best way to convince her nothing had changed and how she should continue being the besotted fool who had adored him.

Grief, shame and yearning had her turning her head away from the sight of him as much as away from her memories, only to experience a sharp pain in her head. Gasping, she lifted her hands and felt . . . bandages.

"Vincent? Vincent!"

He leaned over her, grasped both her wrists and drew her hands against his chest. "Hush. It's all right. Listen to me, Ceara. You're going to be fine."

"What have they done to me? Oh, my God... get me out. I have to get out."

"Darling, be still. You'll only hurt yourself more," he said, bowing his head to press kisses on her clenched fists.

She realized her mistake the moment she heard his endearment, and when she grew aware of the heat and strength of his powerful body emanating through his black turtleneck sweater. But it was those fervent caresses that sent her tumbling fully into panic. It was recorded on the heart monitor beside her bed, and she felt it over every inch of her trembling body.

A man in a white coat appeared behind Vincent. Although he was a half head shorter, he had a strong build, and to her relief he drew Vincent off the bed and forcibly led him out of the room. By the time he returned with a nurse, Ceara was sitting up, trying to ignore the vertigo overwhelming her and climb out of bed. The doctor and nurse put an easy end to her escape and tucked her back beneath the covers.

"Now, now, Miss Lowell," the doctor said with a congeniality that didn't conceal the concern in his eyes, "you don't want to undo all our good work, do you? My name is Dr. Bernstein. Phil to my prettiest patients. And this is Nan. We've been taking care of you since you were admitted yesterday.''

Yesterday? Unbelievable. Impossible. ''I can't stay,'' she replied, frustrated at how her tongue felt heavy with cement and that she had no strength to fight the hands pressing her down. ''I don't like hospitals.''

''Tell you what, we won't hold it against you if you promise to lie still and cooperate with us.''

Because the pain in her head was excruciating and the dizziness was nauseating her, Ceara did as he asked, although her exasperation and fear remained. ''What's . . . what's wrong with me?''

''You had an accident. Do you remember any of it?''

Concentrating hurt, but she forced herself to try. She recalled something . . . vaguely. The images were mostly flashes and disjointed at best, not unlike a Picasso painting.

She tried harder. Enough of the flashes finally merged to where she recalled an actual scene: she was driving . . . an empty road stretched before her . . . she looked away for a moment to reach for another tissue. Pressure began to grow in Ceara's chest; her head throbbed. She had been crying, feeling as though she might never stop. Even her allergy-sensitive mascara had begun to burn her eyes.

In self-defense she pushed the images away. ''Some,'' she admitted to the man hovering over her.

''It's doubtful you'll ever remember all of it, but you won't mind that, will you?''

He was nice, unthreatening, and Ceara relaxed somewhat. The monitors began to record that, as well. With a murmur of approval, the doctor checked her vital signs. Although he was every bit as dark as Vincent, Ceara noted there were few other similarities between them. Round-faced, and with a receding hairline, if there was anything at all compelling about Phil Bernstein, it was his confidence in his professional ability.

After a while, he drew a penlight from his breast pocket. "Look straight over my shoulder," he directed, pointing the beam into her right eye.

She did, only to settle her gaze inadvertently on Vincent, who filled the doorway, watching them. The look on his face was primal and ready for violence.

Even as a shiver raced through her, Ceara averted her gaze. Phil Bernstein glanced over his shoulder. When he turned back to her, his expression was sympathetic. "He certainly makes a strong impression, doesn't he?"

That, Ceara thought, was the understatement of a lifetime.

"You want to talk about it? Him? Anything?"

"No."

"He's been worried sick about you. Acted like a madman when he first arrived."

"Guilt."

"Ouch." He sat back and eyed her with surprise and growing admiration. "For someone who doesn't look as if she'd hurt a mosquito, you're turning out to be one tough customer."

Ceara attempted a grimace, but her facial muscles were so sore, the result was more of a wince. "It's the new me." But old habits die hard, and she soon regretted her bluntness. "I didn't...I don't mean to be rude."

A warm smile lit Phil Bernstein's eyes. "You weren't. Try looking toward the left. You'll love the view. It's an entirely unthreatening wall. Great...now to the right."

"Doctor, was...was surgery necessary?" Ceara asked, focusing on the nurse who was adjusting knobs and dials. She had lost her mother on an operating table when she was seven. The thought of having been in the same predicament filled her with horror.

"No. But you have a nasty cut inside your hairline up here," he said, indicating the location on his own head. "And you suffered a severe concussion. You had us concerned about how long you were intending to stay unconscious."

He asked her several more questions gauged to monitor her memory and linguistic abilities. She answered them all despite a growing fatigue.

"When can I leave?" she asked, her eyelids winning the battle and slowly but surely cutting her vision. All she could see was the doctor's pen stop midway through scribbling notes on her chart.

"My dear, if you tried to stand right now, you'd fall right on that pert nose of yours, not to mention undo our nice sewing job. How about asking me again in a few days?"

Days? She couldn't possibly stay here that long. But somehow she couldn't form the words, nor could she escape the pull of darkness. Soon she stopped trying.

"Well?"

"She's rather upset with you, isn't she?" Phil Bernstein countered as he emerged from the unit.

Vincent clenched his hands into fists but managed to hold on to his temper. "I was referring to her medical condition. How is she?"

"If she continues to improve, we'll move her to a private room later today. Then we'll see." He pocketed his pen and eyed him with what Vincent decided was more than a touch of satisfaction. "Your presence doesn't have a positive effect on her. Will you consider leaving?"

"I will not. Next question."

The doctor sighed. "You don't seem to understand the rules, Dante. I gave you the benefit of the doubt before because I didn't know what we were dealing with. With Ceara regaining consciousness all old deals are off. Just seeing you had her sending those machines in there running haywire, so give me one good reason why I shouldn't call for security and have you thrown out of here."

Ah, Vincent thought, *now it was 'Ceara,' was it?* At the same time he had to ask himself why he was surprised when he had been no less enchanted by and possessive toward her upon *their* first meeting? He lifted his gaze to the ceiling and shook his head. "You ask for too much. You also have no idea how vulnerable my absence would make her to the press. The most innocent of conversations between her and one of your staff could wind up in some sleazy tabloid. No, Doctor, not only will I not share our personal...differences with you, I won't delegate her protection to strangers, either."

"You're not leaving me with much choice."

He knew that; he just didn't know what to do about it. Swearing silently, he rubbed at the permanent lines between his eyebrows. "Wait a minute," he said as something came to mind. "Has she actually asked you to send me away?"

The shorter man hesitated but finally admitted, "Maybe not in so many words..."

Relief and hope, Vincent thought, drawing and exhaling a deep breath, were remarkably rejuvenating. "Then what's to say you aren't being premature? Give her time to think things through. Later, if she asks me to go, I'll reconsider. But not before."

He watched as Ceara's doctor dealt with his suggestion. Clearly the man wasn't used to having his authority challenged, but that was the least of his concerns. No one knew Ceara better than he did, and he was convinced her reactions had been a response to shock, along with an inadequate amount of time to analyze and come to terms with what admittedly had been a disturbing revelation. Once she'd had an opportunity to think things through, however, she would understand and see the wisdom in his and Carson's actions.

His future depended on that.

Concentrate. Once again Ceara smoothed the sheet and blanket over her lap and tried to rehearse what she intended to say to Vincent. He would be arriving at any moment; she knew it as surely as she had memorized the visiting schedule. She was also certain that this time she wouldn't be able to put him off by pretending to be asleep. There was too much intimacy in these private rooms. She had discovered as much last night after being moved in here. His propensity for touching her—the fleeting caress of fingers across her cheek, or the tender squeeze of her hand—had created an atmosphere of sheer torture, accentuating her vulnerability to him. No, she had to be straightforward about this. But how was she going to convince him to go away and stay out of her life when it was only the practical side of her that wanted that?

By the time the door opened and Vincent swept into the room, Ceara was an emotional wreck, wishing whatever followed would be anticlimactic. Her heart, however, knowing nothing about high drama, raced like a sprinter finding herself in a marathon. Strange how it could behave so when on a wholly cerebral level she was working at trying to despise him calmly and methodically.

It was obvious he had gone home to freshen up; the whiskers were gone, his hair was combed back into his usual conservative side-parted sweep and he was wearing a gray turtleneck and slacks instead of the black she remembered seeing when she first regained consciousness yesterday.

"You're sitting up—that's marvelous!"

His rich baritone sent currents of pleasure through her and raised goose bumps on her arms. She resisted the impulse to rub them away, instead focusing on her feelings of injustice and betrayal. "I'm only bruised, not crippled," she replied stiffly.

As she expected, his engaging smile wilted and the light in his eyes dimmed. What surprised her, however, was her reaction to his hurt. Her resolve withered like a blossom under a hot desert sun. Feeling thoroughly rotten, she belatedly nodded at his raincoat. Who wore one with more panache? "It's, um, still raining, I see."

After a slight hesitation, he shrugged off the moisture-beaded covering and, glancing around, laid it over the vinyl chair in the corner. "Fall's arrived even if the calendar disagrees."

Ceara collected her floundering courage. "You shouldn't have come back this morning. I . . . I appreciate your sense of obligation, but—"

"Don't be absurd."

She shouldn't have been surprised at his dismissal of her rehearsed speech. As far as she could tell, he had always lived by only one set of rules: his own. Still, she couldn't, wouldn't continue to make it easy for him. "Vincent, I meant what I said yesterday."

"Yesterday you barely knew your own name." He rounded the bed and sat down by her left knee. His expression gentled. "How are you feeling this morning? You look wonderful."

Ceara leaned farther back into her pillows, fighting the urge to do the opposite—to throw herself into his arms. "I look like a human punching bag. I'm getting a black eye, and as you once succinctly pointed out, black doesn't suit me."

"Correction," he drawled, his expression turning wry. "I said it didn't suit your age. You were barely eighteen then, and the gown you wanted was hardly what Carson had in mind for your first formal. If you wore it today, you'd be—irresistible."

Unable to remain immune to the magnetic pull of his eyes, Ceara focused on the white spider chrysanthemums he had brought for her yesterday evening. He never forgot anything, including her love for any variety of white flower.

Concentrate.

"Vincent . . . we need to talk."

Though she could feel him stiffen, he inclined his head. "I realize that, but you're hardly in any condition—"

"Will you please stop patronizing me!" Her sharpness startled even her, and she bowed her head to avoid seeing either his hurt or annoyance. "I'm sorry. But you must understand. Everything has changed."

"Only in your mind. I'm trying to help you, Ceara. It's never been my intention to patronize—or manipulate."

She laughed briefly and without humor. "No, of course not. Vincent, it's so ingrained in you, you're not even aware you do it. But I'm not without blame myself," she continued, lowering her gaze to the folded hands in her lap. "I've always been too eager to please ... and gullible."

"You're making yourself sound like Milquetoast."

She cautiously lifted her least sore shoulder in a half shrug. "Whatever I was, it's important to make you understand I'm no longer that person. From here on I intend to take control of my own life."

He stared at her for a seemingly endless time before rising and pacing the width of the room. "This is still about what you read in your father's journals," he muttered at last.

"And why not? Anyone with an ounce of intelligence and a respect for free will would take it as an affront if they'd suddenly learned their futures had been decided for them. You and my father were wrong, Vincent, and that truth will stand between us for the rest of our lives, just...just as it would have between Dad and I if he hadn't died." Because her voice had begun to shake from her contained passion, she paused to moisten her lips. "But there's even more to this than your collusion. The accident has had a profound impact on me."

"It has on me, as well."

Ceara forced herself to dismiss the questions his statement spawned, reminding herself that she could no longer afford to care. "I've been thinking of what a close call it was."

"What were you doing driving up here, Ceara? Where were you going?"

"I don't know. I just needed to get out of the apartment. Instead I ... I almost killed myself. A reality like that has a tendency to make you review your life. What I saw in mine didn't impress me."

Vincent grunted his dismissal. "You've always been your own severest critic."

"With good cause," Ceara insisted. "I spent the past seven years of my life sleepwalking through school and halfheartedly fulfilling my obligations at the publishing house because I was trying to please my father. But what I'm most ashamed of," she added quietly, "is making a fool of myself over you. When I think of how tedious it must have been for you . . ."

"I'm not going to listen to this." Vincent stopped at the foot of her bed and, resting his hands on the metal footboard, leaned toward her. "It was nothing of the kind. You were never anything less than warm and sincere and . . . loving. You start to apologize for that and then I'd have to apologize for being human, which won't happen, because I treasure those years, Ceara. I *wanted* every crumb of attention you gave me."

"'Every?' I think not. If you did, you would never have made a covenant with my father."

Vincent's answering sigh made him sound like someone carrying the weight of the world on his shoulders. "It was the right thing to do. At the time you were eighteen and I was thirty-seven. Good Lord, I was—*am* old enough to be your father!"

"But you're not my father, nor did I ever think of you in that vein. Of course, if you think of me as the daughter you've never had . . ."

"You know damn well I don't," he ground out.

It wasn't much, but Ceara allowed herself a moment to cherish the admission for old time's sake. "Well, you could have fooled me. At any rate, if your entire argument hinges on age," she continued doggedly, "it's groundless."

His answering smile was grim. "Your determination to argue the point proves otherwise."

Stung, Ceara swallowed the lump lodged in her throat. It was clear he was angry with himself over having made the confession and was now out to reclaim lost ground, but to do so at the cost of hurting her? She lifted her chin. "Age has nothing to do with feelings. Accept it, Vincent, you were wrong. Just as you and my father were wrong to discuss your relationship with me behind my back." She closed her eyes against the anguish that was still bitter and sharp. "My God . . . to be dealt with like some . . . some inconvenience. I could almost hate you."

"Ceara." Vincent came around the bed and sat down again, this time taking her clenched hands within his. "Don't say such things. You don't mean them."

"Oh, yes, I'm afraid I do."

"You're still suffering from shock."

"On the contrary, I've never felt more clearheaded in my life. Don't look so dour," she added, forcing a flippancy into her voice she hardly felt. "You should be congratulating yourself. After all, this is what you wanted, isn't it? To be rid of me? At least as a clinging vine?"

He sat back as if she had slapped him. "I beg your pardon?"

"For someone who's often complimented on his ability to untangle the most complicated plots, you're being suspiciously slow. I'm telling you that you've gotten your wish. You no longer need to feel burdened with my unwanted affections. I plan to. . . to explore my horizons and concentrate on reaching my full potential as an independent woman."

When he continued to merely stare at her, Ceara tried another shrug. "All right, maybe that did sound like a ladies' cigarette ad. However, the sentiment fits. It cost me a brand-new car, but I learned a good lesson from my accident, Vincent. I realize now that I spent the first twenty-five years of my life being a shadow of what I could be. I was my father's dutiful daughter, his hostess, his companion and employee...even his nurse in the end. Oh, I don't resent him for it. Mother's death was as hard on him as it was on me. It was natural for us to cling to each other. But there should have come a time when he learned to let go. Obviously he didn't— just as you didn't learn to take what was right before your eyes. So now I'm going to live for *me*."

She dared lift her gaze to meet Vincent's because she needed to know how he was taking all this. He sat there unblinking, his bearing stiff and still.

"I would never ask anyone to be less than all they could be," he said slowly.

"I knew you'd understand."

"The question is, now what?"

"Well, in a way nothing," she said with a feigned casualness. "I go on with my life and you go on with yours. We'll stay in touch, of course, though we both know what a recluse you are at heart. I know standing by me during Dad's funeral cost you a lot. I'll always be grateful." She gestured, uncomfortably aware of desperation tightening her vocal cords. "Maybe you'll come to the city for Christmas. You've said it's at its most tolerable then. We can plan to have dinner."

"By which time you'll have mastered an hour or two's worth of empty chatter to keep things from getting too awkward between us. Is that the plan, Ceara? To reduce me to the ranks of those stuffed shirts and bores you entertained for your father at his dinner parties?''

As he spoke, he leaned forward, forcing her to press back against the pillows. "They weren't all—no, of course not. I only..."

"Want to hurt me...as I've hurt you. I can understand that. But you also want to get me out of your life," he said, leaning even closer so that he loomed over her, bracing his weight on hands he had placed on either side of her. "Do you think I'm going to let you?"

She couldn't think at all when he was this close. His after-shave, a subdued woodsy scent she could call to memory even when she hadn't seen him in weeks, intoxicated her senses. His eyes burned into her and his mouth...her blood grew feverish with yearning to know it in passion as she had experienced it during friendly, chaste kisses.

"What a fascinating, traitorous face you have," he murmured, scanning each of her features again and again. "Emotions and thoughts cross it like fleeting clouds over a brilliant moon. You made your tidy speech with such confidence, yet you're really as nervous as a titmouse. You've declared your independence, but there are tears burning in the back of your eyes. No, Ceara, inside and out you can't be anything but what you are—all honest passion and sweet desire waiting to be tapped. Do you have any idea how badly I've wanted to be the man to explore those sides of you?"

"Vincent, let me be," she entreated, her heart beginning to pound and her resistance slipping fast. "I'm not feeling well."

"Well enough to turn my world upside down. Well enough to try to cast me out of your life like an old, worn shoe."

"Poignant words for a man who found it easy enough to resist me and my numerous charms for seven years!"

Nothing hit him as hard as the truth. Vincent sat up, his own face a complex study of anger and something Ceara refused to let herself analyze. A vein in his right temple pulsed, further exposing his agitation and his wide, firm mouth flattened into a grim line.

"Ceara," he began, his voice strained, "you can't begin to understand how complicated all this is."

She was spared having to think of a suitable comment thanks to Phil Bernstein's arrival.

"At it again, I see," he drawled.

Vincent came off the bed like a pouncing leopard. "You see *nothing*, Doctor."

Ceara decided either her physician was a superb actor or else he didn't intimidate as easily as most people did around Vincent. Brushing by him, the doctor replied, "I feel I've stepped into a modern-day rendition of Beauty and the Beast. Dante, be a good fellow and stop growling at my patient. Good morning, Ceara. How's this, that and the other?"

Though she was grateful for his irreverent humor, it was his reassuring wink she appreciated the most. "Considering my options, Doctor, how can I complain? The headache is worsening, though."

"Why didn't you say something before?" Vincent demanded, immediately at her side.

"The subject didn't come up."

"Give her something, Bernstein," he ordered, his tone leaving no room for contradiction. "I won't have her in pain."

"Won't you?" Phil Bernstein sighed and sat down on the spot Vincent had vacated. "I don't suppose it's occurred to you that she'd probably get more relief if she was allowed some rest?"

"What I'd like to do is go home," Ceara told him.

His answering look was skeptical. "I've been studying your chart. You need another few days of complete bed rest."

"I can get it there. We have . . . I have a live-in house-keeper," she explained. But mentioning Mrs. Green only reminded her of how empty the place was going to seem without her father around. Despite his flaws he had been such a dynamic man, larger than life and not unlike Vincent, though in a less mysterious way.

Phil Bernstein remained silent, reading the reports of her progress as though they alone held the verdict of her fate. She couldn't let it hinge on them. If she stayed here, she would never be able to avoid Vincent; and if she couldn't at least keep some distance between them, her plan to wean herself away from needing and caring for him was going to fail miserably.

"Considering what I told you about how much I dislike hospitals, I'd think you'd understand how much faster I would recuperate in my own home," she persisted.

"That's the only point running in your favor." But his glance told her he remained reluctant to let her go. "Mind telling me how you propose getting there? You're certainly not going to get behind the wheel of a car for another week or two."

"I'll take her, of course," Vincent replied.

"That's . . . that's not necessary," Ceara injected. She forced herself to look at him. "You've already done more than enough. It would be no problem to phone someone from the office, or I could call a cab."

"You'll walk across Antarctica barefoot," Vincent muttered, clearly agitated at having this disagreement before a stranger. "For pity's sake, Ceara, if you don't want to speak to me, all you have to do is pretend to be asleep again. I can take a hint, but I *will* be driving you back to Manhattan."

He had known! She should have guessed; the man wasn't human. Mrs. Green had often said as much herself after his visits to their home. He had never been or done anything like other people. He could tell she had been trying to hide from him!

And now he was challenging her to deal with her fear of him, her fear of being around him and that of betraying her true feelings about their relationship. Yet at the same time, if ever she had been presented with an opportunity to convince him once and for all how she had indeed changed, of how strong and determined she could be, this was it. But, oh, the cost if she didn't succeed. Did she dare risk it?

Like Phil Bernstein, he was waiting for her reply, his dark, intense gaze enigmatic. Hypnotic. Ceara gripped the bed covers and wet her dry lips. "All right," she said, her voice husky but clear. "Thank you, Vincent. If you've the time to spare, I would be grateful for a ride home."

Chapter Three

For the first thirty minutes of the trip they drove in silence. Vincent didn't mind; he needed time to recover from his earlier conversation with Ceara. Not since he had been a rash college student had he come this close to casting discretion to the wind and yielding completely to impulse—and he was a much more disciplined person now. It was as annoying as it was disturbing; and if he was to repair any of the damage done by Carson's journals, regain Ceara's confidence and trust, he had to make sure he didn't push himself too close to an emotional edge again.

Only how much of their friendship could he risk recovering? At what point would he bring them beyond that emotional crossroads from which there was no turning back? Was he really willing to deal with everything if they went beyond it?

Damn those journals. He should have known Carson would keep meticulous records. His friend had been as much an historian as he was a perfectionist; he hadn't trusted anyone else to review his life, at least not without giving him or her explicit notes to follow. Vincent kept no such records himself; the past, as far as he was concerned, could and should be left to rot when he did. He harbored no desire for anyone to pry into his life. His successes were recorded on various bestseller lists, and his mistakes and failures were his alone to ruminate over and judge. After all, he was the one serving penance for them.

Had Carson given any forethought to the difficulties he was creating with those painstaking documentaries? If they ever got into the wrong hands, the media would have a field day with them; and even though she was innocent of everything, Ceara would suffer the most from the piranhas' frenzied attacks. Consideration should have been given to that. Why hadn't Carson done so?

What else was in them? Did he write down everything? God, Vincent moaned inwardly, he should never have succumbed to that last cognac the night he ended up confiding his darkest secret. No doubt it had served to add to Carson's concern about his relationship with his daughter. Who wouldn't have been disconcerted? Though he felt his friend would have asked for the promise regardless of his past. Ceara was right there; Carson had coveted the attentions of his only child for himself. That confession had done nothing more than accelerate the request.

Vincent sighed. The skies were gray again this morning, but the roadways had dried after yesterday's rains. The worst of the morning traffic was easing; however, the closer they got to the city, the more he had to drive defensively.

"Can you actually see yourself taking a grimy cab and tolerating who knows what through this?" he demanded of Ceara, incensed at the mere thought.

"I already thanked you."

Her listless reply had him shooting her a quick glance, and his heart contracted at what he saw. She looked like a broken doll that the seat belt alone was keeping from slumping over. Not even the soft mauve sweater dress he had gone out and purchased for her because her own clothes were bloodied and torn added any color to her shockingly pale face.

"You should still be in the hospital," he muttered, changing lanes and accelerating with new fervor. The more quickly he got her home, the sooner Mrs. Green could get her tucked into bed. The woman was a hag, but he couldn't fault her devotion to Ceara; she would see to her proper care.

"I couldn't sleep there, you know that."

"Thank you for finally allowing me to drive you."

Her laugh was barely more than an expulsion of breath. "Did you give me a choice?"

"If it's a crime to be concerned about the well-being of someone one cares about, then I'm guilty."

"What you are is an autocrat, just as my father was, and why I didn't see it years ago, I'll never know."

"Would you like me to tell you?" he replied, smiling with cynicism but regretting that those days were lost to them forever. When she didn't reply, he decided to continue, anyway. "Because back then you looked at me, at both of us, through the rose-tinted glasses of an innocent."

"Don't remind me."

Although he deserved all her sarcasm and more, he couldn't help asking, "I've destroyed your trust in me, haven't I?"

"You'll understand if I fail to see the need to answer you."

"By all means, go ahead. Anything is better than this oppressive silence that's fallen between us . . . even your wrath."

"I'm too tired to try to match wits with you, Vincent."

He swore at himself for adding to her fatigue and stress. Could he do nothing right? He shot her another glance. Bernstein had removed the bandages around her head and replaced them with a square of taped gauze covering only the stitches. The nurses had washed her long hair for her and blow-dried it; the ash-brown tresses fell over her shoulders like a silk mantle completely covering her small high breasts.

"Are you warm enough?" Her own raincoat had been among the things ruined, and she had stubbornly refused to take his, insisting she didn't need it going from the wheelchair to his car, which he had parked at the front door of the hospital. To him she was a will-o'-the-wisp; she didn't look capable of generating enough body warmth to keep herself alive. "I can turn up the heat."

"It isn't necessary."

He scowled at the traffic before them and Manhattan's skyline in the distance. She was shutting him out and it hurt. He wondered if she knew how much, or did she even care? "I phoned Mrs. Green to let her know we were on our way."

"Did she happen to mention how her granddaughter was?"

"No, why? Is something the matter with her?"

"She's been ill. The doctors don't seem to know what's wrong. A fourteen-month-old can't very well tell you why and where she's hurting. I was hoping there might have been news by now."

How like Ceara, he thought. Always thinking of someone else's health and welfare before her own. Mrs. Green's daughter lived in Arizona, and while the distance was no doubt something hard to deal with, Ceara was more sensitive to it than he expected many employers would be.

"I'm sorry I didn't know to ask."

What was unnecessary to explain was that he and Mrs. Green didn't get along well enough for him to broach personal subjects. She had been with the Lowells for longer than he had known them, and from the beginning she had made it clear she had more than a few reservations about him. A canny woman, Vincent thought with droll humor.

"You might be relieved to know I did speak with Derrick Moreland," he said, referring to the new editor in chief of Lowell Publishing. "He sent you his best and said not to worry about rushing back to work. He even suggested you might want to take some time off."

"I'm surprised he didn't suggest I resign entirely and live off my inheritance until I found something I really wanted to do."

Her acerbic tone and the admission was so surprising, Vincent wasn't sure he had heard correctly. "I thought you liked being an editor?"

"I *like* books. It was my father who wanted me to be an editor. He felt it was a good starting point to groom me for the day I'd take over the company, or at least sit on the board. Unfortunately I found that a fondness for reading and an appropriate degree does not necessarily a good editor make. More often than not, I'm tempted to suggest aspiring writers take up another pastime, any pastime than the one they're dabbling in. I don't find it an adventure to wade through stacks of submissions in the hopes of finding one potential jewel. It breaks my heart to see a good but not great book passed over because the budget to acquire it just isn't there. I've no stomach for the prima dons and donnas of the industry who think their words came from God's lips to their ears, nor for the lesson that the squeakiest wheel gets the most oil. I love books,'' she finished sadly, "but I wasn't cut out to make them shine.''

Vincent would have reached over, taken her hand and brought it to his lips if he thought she would let him get away with the gesture. It was the most personal insight about herself that she had shared with him in days, and she couldn't begin to know how starved he was for the morsel.

He had guessed all wasn't going well for her at work, and wondered if it couldn't be the work load or perhaps a problem with one of her colleagues, although she had seemed to be getting along with them as well as she did with most people. What would be her ultimate decision? Carson's death gave her a clear path out; however, at the same time it burdened her with a yoke of responsibility she might succumb to out of respect for his memory.

"I can't tell you how relieved I am to hear you say that,'' he told her. When he felt her sidelong look, he shrugged. "It was obvious the light and laughter were slowly being suffocated out of you. If you haven't found your niche yet, keep searching for it.''

"Easy words for you to say.''

"Meaning?"

"I don't have other brothers or sisters to fill my space if I did decide to turn my back on my father's business."

"Understood. But by the same token you don't owe Carson your life. You're your own person with a right to make your own decisions."

He could almost feel her stiffen beside him. "Is that how you see me? As someone who's being sacrificial?"

"What would you call it?"

"Having a strong sense of tradition."

"All right, accepted. But even so, you face the same conflict—obligation and the price it demands. Complicate the issue with love, and people can be made to do strange things," he replied, reflecting back on his own life. Could she possibly understand? She should, considering her relationship with Carson had been one of total devotion. But she might only want to see so far. If half that devotion had belonged to *him,* he could win a modicum of it back; he was certain of it. Unfortunately, no doubt his portion of her heart had been much smaller.

Silence returned and reigned for the rest of the trip. When Vincent arrived at her apartment building, he parked in the private garage, using Ceara's pass to get inside. Then, without giving her a chance to protest, he draped his coat over her shoulders and assisted her to the elevator. He would have preferred sweeping her into his arms and carrying her, and would have—if he hadn't believed she would use whatever energy she had left to fight him. It was just as well, because he didn't trust himself. He couldn't touch Ceara without wanting her, and giving in to that want, even slightly, could destroy whatever communication there remained between them.

Her apartment was on the fifteenth floor, not quite one-third of the way up the tower. When the elevator doors slid open again, they stepped out into the empty hallway that was as sedately elegant as it was quiet. He had learned long ago that most of the building's tenants were like the Lowells—successful people who led busy professional and private lives that either kept them behind their locked doors or out of the place entirely.

Even as Ceara began to slide her key into the dead bolt, the door swung open and an elderly woman wearing a gray-and-white uniform that did nothing for her sallow city complexion reached for her.

"Ceara, child, you've had me so worried about you. How pale you look. Come here now, lean on me and I'll take you straight to your room. I've got some lovely soup ready with—"

"The couch will suit me fine, Mrs. Green," Ceara said, her soft, lilting voice barely audible. "I've had my fill of beds for the moment."

Vincent would have preferred assisting her himself, but the housekeeper usurped his position without sparing him a glance. At five-nine or -ten she was several inches taller than Ceara and easily twice her girth. A broad-faced, no-nonsense woman, she had strong likes and stronger dislikes. That he fell into the latter category didn't bother Vincent, except when it interfered with his desire to be with Ceara.

Fussing over her charge like a fretting chicken, Mrs. Green soon had her settled. "I'll get you some pillows and a blanket. Then I'll bring you a nice tray. Or are you hungry enough to eat first?"

"No, I—" Ceara began.

"What did the doctor say? Should we call our own Dr. Cranston?"

"It's not—"

"There's a prescription to be filled for sure. Ach, your poor head ... and they had to cut some of your hair, I see."

"Mrs. Green," Vincent interrupted, having heard enough to give *him* a migraine. "There's no prescription. Ceara's been advised to take aspirin if necessary. As for calling Dr. Cranston, that would be a waste of time unless an emergency arises. Right now Ceara's in need of a nap more than feeding, since they made her eat a healthy breakfast before they allowed her to check out of the hospital."

Mrs. Green's answering glower could have chipped diamonds. She adjusted the black hair net around her thinning salt-and-pepper hair before returning with, "Allow me to do my job, Mr. Dante. I've been caring for this child for over twelve years, and I assure you she's no less precious to me than if she was my own."

"Please don't upset yourself, Mrs. Green." Ceara squeezed the older woman's hand. "Vincent was running interference for me in the hospital. And he hasn't reminded himself it's no longer necessary," she added, looking pointedly at him. "Why don't you get me the pillows you mentioned and maybe I can have a cup of your wonderful tea?"

No one could take the tension out of a combustible situation faster than Ceara. Vincent watched as Mrs. Green patted her hand and, beaming, assured her that she would be back shortly.

When she was gone, Ceara carefully brushed her hair back from her forehead and cast him another look, this one rife with fatigue. "Must you be so imperious with her?"

"What do you suggest I do, encourage her to treat me like the scourge of the earth, which she already does?"

"You can't fault her for having my best interests at heart."

"And what, pray tell, do you suppose is my motivation?"

Instead of answering she laid her head against the back of the pearl-gray couch and closed her eyes. "Let's table this conversation for another time, shall we? Perhaps during our next incarnation. I'll ask to come back as an Amazon, so I'm better equipped to challenge your domination instincts. In the meantime, why don't you retreat to your tenebrous castle and use all that wasted intellect and cynicism to spin Derrick another best-seller? He'll be so grateful. After all, there's nothing quite like being able to reassure the board of directors that though the king is dead the empire remains sound."

Once again Vincent couldn't believe his ears. Would the shocks never stop coming? What being was this that now spoke with her voice? Ceara, for all her incisive wit and quickness, had never used words as a weapon. Granted, a part of him wanted to leave as she suggested—no one knew better about the solace in solitude than he did—and heaven help him, his soul needed soothing. Yet another, greater, part of him was intrigued, agitated to be sure, but also fascinated with this metamorphosis. He could blame it on his profession— the writer's disease of the blood that compelled him to analyze and dissect—but he couldn't make himself go to the door. A new Ceara was emerging. Out of the wreckage of a European-built steel cocoon was being born a new entity. How could he leave before he fully understood who she had become?

He rose, noting the look of relief that crossed her face. "I'll leave. Soon. But would you mind if I had a drink first?"

Ceara felt as though someone had tugged the sofa out from beneath her. Her stomach plummeted; her heart and lungs followed. She hadn't succeeded, after all. Not only wasn't he going, but the battle of wills was going to continue for yet another round.

"You know your constitution at this hour better than anyone," she replied, hoping she appeared more indifferent than she knew she sounded.

She watched him cross over to the massive antique bar that her father had picked up at an auction years ago. The dark, decidedly baroque piece was an appropriate backdrop to the even more dramatic man. His jaw set in a way he usually saved for the few reporters he deigned to give interviews to, he reached beneath the counter and came up with the sculpted bottle bearing her father's premium Scotch and poured two fingers into one of the crystal tumblers lined on the shelving surrounding the cheval-glass mirror in the background.

"You prefer ice," she reminded him when he came out from behind the bar.

"There isn't any, and I don't think it would be safe to ask Mrs. Green to bring me some right now, would it?"

He reclaimed the high-backed chair beside her. Before them on the coffee table was the gray-and-rose marble chess set. His fleeting glance to it told her that he, too, was remembering how their skirmishes used to be restricted to that battleground. Then he crossed his long legs and took a sip of his drink, seemingly content to eye her over the glistening rim.

In a way she couldn't blame him for his obstinacy. If the tables were turned, would she be any easier to scare away? Still, she wished she was made of stronger stuff; then he would know the full measure of the pain and disappointment she was feeling.

"You spoke of near hate before, but you already do despise me, don't you?" he murmured, lowering his gaze to the amber liquid he swirled in his glass.

"I don't know," she admitted.

He seemed surprised and then strangely buoyed by her response, so that Mrs. Green's return was a double relief to her. Ceara had no idea how she would have responded if pressed for a clarification on what she had just confessed.

"There now," the sturdily built woman said, settling two pillows on one end of the couch. "Now lie back here, set your feet up and I'll tuck you in."

Ceara slipped out of her leather pumps and did as directed, acutely conscious of Vincent's somber study. It was strange, really; he had seen her in tennis clothes and even a bathing suit, yet she had never felt more exposed than she did now.

"Mrs. Green, have you heard from Kit?" she asked, determined to shift attention away from herself. "How's Bonnie?"

The craggy lines around her housekeeper's face grew deeper with her frown. "You don't need to be worrying about that, dear."

"But I do. You have heard something, haven't you?"

"Ach, it's sad." Her mummifying of Ceara in the Irish wool throw completed, the housekeeper straightened and clasped her apron between her hands. "Bonnie's going to need surgery, after all. One of her kidneys is failing.''

''How awful. When did you learn this?'' Ceara sat upright, only to experience a sharp pain and dizziness that drew an involuntary gasp from her.

''Now what are you trying to do?'' Mrs. Green scolded.

''Never mind me. Why didn't you tell me about Bonnie sooner?''

''How could I, child? You were in dire straits yourself. I wasn't about to dump my problems on you.''

''It's hardly dumping. You have to—''

The phone rang, cutting her off before she could finish. Mrs. Green hurried over to the unit on the bar and picked up the receiver, formally reciting the greeting she always used when taking family calls. Ceara soon realized it was a reporter, a persistent reporter wanting an interview. Fortunately Mrs. Green was even more tenacious.

''Miss Lowell won't be making any public comments and that's final. Good day,'' the housekeeper said, and returned the receiver to its cradle. No sooner did she accomplish that than the telephone rang again. ''It's been like this ever since news leaked of your accident,'' she told Ceara.

This time it was one of the senior editors at the publishing house. Ceara signaled her that she would take the call; it was one of her favorite co-workers. But she was soon sorry she had been so impulsive because the woman—after asking about her condition—apparently decided the best therapy was to dive into a complete recitation of all the goings-on at the office.

Ceara could feel Vincent's gaze boring into her, and she was surprised he didn't snatch the receiver from her grasp and give her friend a piece of his mind. "Lena," she said, finally deciding she was at the end of her own endurance, "let me call you back in a few days? I'm just home and I still feel somewhat queasy. What...? No, of course you didn't overdo it... Okay, bye."

As soon as she hung up, Mrs. Green moved the telephone back to its proper place. "I've a good mind to unplug every one. I would have if I wasn't anxious about getting a call from you and my Kit."

"Speaking of Kit," Ceara said, trying to avoid rubbing her aching head, "don't you think it would help her if you were with her?"

"And what about you?"

"She's your daughter, Mrs. Green," Ceara insisted, touched that the woman could be so torn by her loyalties. "You must put your family first."

"If things were different, maybe. But with your father only recently gone and now this accident... Ceara, child, I'll admit that I was thinking of retiring and moving to Arizona to be with Kit and the family, but look at you. You're in no condition to be abandoned."

The news came as more of a surprise than it should have. Back when Kit and her new husband had moved west, Ceara told herself it was inevitable that one day Mrs. Green would follow; yet it still came as a blow. It took much of her remaining strength to summon a smile. "You helped raise me to be more durable than that, Livvy," she said, using the affectionate abbreviation of her name, which her father had indulged in at holidays and special moments. "I'll be fine. I want you to—"

The ringing phone interrupted them again. This time Vincent motioned for Mrs. Green to stay where she was and took the call himself. He managed to get rid of whoever it was by simply hanging up after replying a curt, "No interviews."

"Call the airline and Kit, then pack your things," Ceara said to the housekeeper as Vincent rejoined them. "I'll be fine."

"With everyone and their cousin tying up the phone and ringing the call box?" Mrs. Green thrust out her lower lip and shook her head. "I wouldn't be able to forgive myself."

"Think of your daughter," Ceara insisted. "She needs help. Just last week you made a comment about how difficult it was for her to keep an eye on the boys and care for Bonnie, too."

"We'll discuss it again in a week or two when you're feeling more like your old self."

"And in the meantime you'll get an ulcer worrying about how they're coping in Arizona. Make the calls. You're going to be with those that need you the most."

"*No,* I say. Not while I know you're alone."

"She won't be alone," Vincent said quietly. "I'll be with her."

Both Ceara and her housekeeper shot him startled looks. Mrs, Green, however, was the first to recover. "Hell will grow mushrooms first, Mr. Dante."

He lifted his glass in salute. "As always, madam, your warmth and goodwill is touching."

"Vincent, stop it," Ceara beseeched before turning back to the older woman. "He can take you to the airport on his way home. Don't worry."

"I don't recall yielding my right to speak for myself," Vincent told her. "Though I'll take her—and gladly," he added, shooting a feral smile at the indignant woman. "But unless you can change the locks on the doors while I'm gone, I'll be back, because for once she's right. You can't be left alone."

"Then I'll call a friend to come stay with me."

"Who? That gossip who just phoned? I think not."

"Vincent," Ceara ground out, beginning to lose patience. "May I point out this isn't a decision that's yours to make?"

"You have two options," he said, annoyingly calm as he extended a thumb and index finger. "Either I stay here or you come back to my estate with me."

"She'll do no such thing," Mrs. Green huffed in reply. She spun back to Ceara. "I knew it. He's up to no good. A regular Rasputin, that's what he is. A Svengali casting his spells to get what he wants. Oh, I warned Mr. Lowell, God rest his soul. I told him that it wasn't normal for an eccentric with this one's grim nature to seek out the company of anyone possessing your youth and vitality. Send him away," she insisted, clasping Ceara's hands within her own. "It's for your own good, child."

Ceara barely heard her; she was busy reading the messages telegraphed via Vincent's sizzling gaze. No, she knew he wouldn't leave, just as he knew she wouldn't cause a scene and have him thrown out by security. The history between them went back too far and was too deep to resort to the interference of any more third parties. At the same time that didn't mean she was ready to submit to his bullying.

There was a knock at the door. All three of them glanced at one another in momentary confusion. Usually no one made it upstairs without first getting clearance from the doorman. Mrs. Green went to the door and peered through the security hole.

"Flowers," she said, unbolting the dead bolt.

As soon as she began opening the door, a wiry, burr-haired young man pushed inside. He thrust the flower arrangement he was carrying into the housekeeper's hands under which he had been holding a camera. "Ms. Lowell, I'm with the—"

He never got farther. Vincent lunged at him as though shot from a cannon. Grabbing the man by the scruff of his collar before he could even take one photograph, he literally carried him out to the hall. "Try that again and you'd better have extensive insurance coverage," he growled, slamming the door. As soon as he secured the dead bolt, he spun around to face Ceara. "Your options have just experienced a fifty percent cutback."

"I'm calling the police," Mrs. Green declared, heading for the phone.

"No, wait." As she spoke, Ceara didn't take her eyes off Vincent. He wasn't bluffing. She had no doubt that he would stay—or snatch her off the couch and carry her out to his car. But be with her he would, whether she liked it or not. In which case, she decided, she would rather go to his home. At least there she could always hope he would eventually lock himself in his study and focus on his writing. "I'll go with you," she told him, her gaze as steady as his. "But it's to be understood that this is temporary."

"Contrary to what Mrs. Green thinks, the walls and gates that surround my estate are to keep intruders out, not guests in."

"And you understand this acquiescence is that and nothing else?"

"Afraid I'll be tempted to seduce you?" he replied with equal grimness.

Mrs. Green gasped. "Mr. Dante!"

"Calm yourself," Vincent replied, ignoring her. "Even if you can't find it in your heart to trust me, my houseman is from the old school. Your honor and privacy will be as certain as if you were cloistering yourself in a medieval nunnery."

"Anyone foolish enough to believe that deserves what they get," Mrs. Green scoffed.

Vincent's gaze grew more compelling, making it impossible for Ceara to break their hold. "Trust me, Ceara," he said more gently. "You know you want to."

She did. That was the unsettling part of it all. She wanted to yield to him and find solace in his reassurances, as well as in his arms. The question was what price would she pay this time if she discovered she had made a terrible mistake?

Chapter Four

Regardless of how upset Ceara was with him, Vincent felt a distinct euphoria as the electronic gates closed behind them and he drove up the circuitous, leaf-littered drive to the house. He was bringing Ceara to his home. He had fantasized about the moment so often, he wasn't sure he wasn't dreaming now. But, no, he assured himself as he cast her a brief glance, in none of his visions had she ever looked this pensive or resentful.

At least the weather was cooperating. Although the early-afternoon sun was behind the long-reaching branches hanging over the drive, its bright rays turned the amber and russet leaves to the richer tones of brass and bronze. After days of rain, the crisp air made everything look sharp and clear, while a persistent breeze nudged and tossed the fallen leaves across the roadway as if they were mischievously cavorting children.

The grounds, too, were hardly the manicured setting typical of an estate this size; however, to Vincent, that was part of its attraction. He didn't want trimmed hedges and uniform flower beds; he wanted the primitive appeal of the wilderness surrounding him so that no matter from what window he looked out he saw nature at its most natural and honest.

As a result, the undergrowth was thick and entangled by assorted vines and briars; the evergreens were bent in mysterious shapes, their trunks craning and twisting in an ongoing quest to gain a superior glimpse of the sun. In a way, they provided him with twice as much privacy, creating a living barrier inside the man-made wall. Security-wise and aesthetically it was, he thought, the most fitting encasement. He knew he was right the moment they rounded the last bend and Ceara spotted his home for the first time in her life.

Her breath caught. That much he expected. One's initial glimpse of the three-storied stone structure was a close-up view, and that only reinforced feelings of wondering if one had somehow journeyed back to another century. But what fascinated and thrilled him was seeing that rather than shivering or recoiling from the sight, Ceara leaned forward and pressed her hand to the windshield.

Fascination, not fear. Could he have asked for a greater gift—except perhaps to have been given permission to show it to her sooner?

Slightly over a hundred years old, the house had been built by someone who had been inspired and torn between Norman and Gothic architecture. High, spiky dormers rose from the third floor, two of which looked over the second-story balcony buttressed by matching stone and heavy wooden beams that reached across the driveway to create a protective, multiarched portico high enough for almost any size vehicle to drive under. At the top of the house five chimneys rose from the steep, sloping roof and billowy puffs of smoke trailed out of two, indicating Townsend had been busy since receiving his call yesterday afternoon. The smoke from the one on the left meant there was a cheerful blaze in the living room fireplace awaiting them, and the steady but thinner trail from the other in the back meant his houseman was preparing a lavish dinner in the kitchen's modernized brick oven.

"It's everything Dad said it was," Ceara said, her voice so low Vincent knew she was speaking to herself. "And more."

Upon his invitation, Carson had come here several times, and with each visit he had reiterated how Ceara would love the place. But his friend had preferred keeping her away, admitting the house would undoubtedly have as strong an effect on her as its owner did and, therefore, was an unwise move. Naturally Vincent had been disappointed that he couldn't share this most personal part of himself with her. Now, he thought as he parked inside the portico, he would finally have his chance.

No sooner did he shut off the engine and climb out than the solid oak double front doors opened and a tall, distinguished-looking man emerged. Only his houseman, Vincent mused, could remain looking dignified while being caught with his dress shirt's sleeves rolled up and wearing a chef's apron.

"Hello, Townsend," he murmured to the Englishman whose long, gaunt-cheeked face looked as if it were carved from tallow. "Busy in the kitchen, I see."

"I thought that under the circumstances something special was in order, sir. The beef Wellington will be ready at seven."

Vincent raised an eyebrow. He only rarely allowed his houseman to fuss over him and even then he preferred a simple steak and salad to fancier fare. Townsend was, however, correct; this was a special occasion. "I'm impressed. No doubt you've already been down in the cellar to choose an appropriate wine?"

"A red Bordeaux. Perhaps not as lighthearted as some of your Beaujolais, but with the cool, damp nights we've been having, I had Miss Lowell's fragile state of health in mind."

"Thank you, Townsend. If you'll see to her bags, I'll assist her inside."

By the time he rounded the front of the car, Ceara had already climbed out; but she had tried to move with her usual speed and he could see that while the spirit was willing, the body remained weak. As she gripped the doorframe to steady herself, he slipped his arm around her waist. "Dizzy?"

She stiffened at his touch and avoided his searching gaze. "I'm sure it will pass in a moment."

"Nonsense."

Whatever color she had regained since leaving the hospital was gone, and despite a good night's sleep there were new shadows under her eyes. She didn't look strong enough to slam the door she was hanging on to, let alone capable of dealing with all the stairs and hallways that awaited her inside. Unwilling to let her risk even trying, he lifted her into his arms.

"Vincent!"

"All this driving over the past two days has drained you. Bernstein would have my head if he saw how you look."

"I only need a moment to get used to having my feet beneath me again."

"Tomorrow will be soon enough to start dealing with that."

Although she had no choice but to slip her arms around his neck and hold on, she continued to avoid any eye contact and kept her head lowered. "You're embarrassing me."

"Considering what else I'm guilty of, it's a small offense, don't you think?" he muttered, responding to the ache deep inside him. How he wished she was in his arms for an entirely different reason. "At least some color's returning to your cheeks. We can't have you frightening Townsend. He's English enough to believe that every time the power goes off or the wind makes the house creak it's a message from the other side. He doesn't need to worry that you're going to add to the spirit world's population."

"What if I reassured him that the only person who'd be in danger of a haunting from me is you?"

"You needn't become a specter to do that," he replied softly. "The pity is after all this time you haven't yet figured that out."

Her cheeks darkening with color as though she had already sipped their dinner wine, Ceara hastily inspected the foyer. Vincent did a slow turn so she could take it in fully, and allowed himself a smile of pleasure when he felt her fingers curl into his shoulders. There was no arguing that the place was a bit on the melodramatic side, but it pleased him to sense her awe and approval.

The foyer was paneled in dark wood; the black marble floors and lacquered exotic furnishings only emphasized the mysterious effect. Instead of mirrors and side tables there were tapestries of medieval knights slaying dragons and alchemists creating magic. In the center of the room was a huge trunk on which was balanced a thick sheet of round-cut glass; and in the middle of it sat a wide brass bowl containing an arrangement made of peacock feathers, pinecones and assorted branches with seed pods and berries, all things growing on the premises.

"I wouldn't be surprised if you told me Merlin's bones were inside that chest," Ceara murmured, staring at the antique chest.

"Someone's could well be, for all I know. The thing was in the cellar when I bought the place and I've never broken the lock to find out what's inside."

"Never! Aren't you curious?"

"Of many things," he murmured, basking in her temporary willingness to communicate with him, just as he relished the feel of her soft curves against him. "But as for that particular item, why ruin the mystery?"

When she looked straight into his eyes, he felt a surge of something powerful and intoxicating seep through his blood. Lord, she was lovely, despite her bruises. Hers was a beauty that began from the inside and radiated outward. The kind that intensified with age.

"Well, what do you think of the place?" he asked, unable to wait a moment longer for her appraisal.

"It's magnificent and compelling and—very much like its owner."

"Thank you." Tempted to say more, to bury his face in the silky mass of hair cascading over her shoulders and his arm, he spun to face his houseman. "Here's the person who deserves all the credit for making everything run smoothly, especially when I'm locked away and concentrating on a book. Townsend, this is Miss Lowell. Why don't you lead the way up to her room?''

After giving Ceara a dignified nod, the older man did as instructed. Vincent had left the choice of rooms up to him, but was pleased that his instincts were on target.

Townsend directed them to the door beside Vincent's own bedroom, murmuring, ''This is the Winter Room, miss. I hope you'll be comfortable here.''

While unlike his room in that it didn't have a fireplace, this one was vastly more luxurious. Vincent had supervised its lavish decorating himself and had chosen the white-on-white effect that was relieved with subtle accents of silver.

Ceara sighed as he carried her over the threshold. ''Oh, put me down,'' she entreated.

He did so only because he was fascinated with her expression and didn't want to do anything that would break the spell. He watched her slip out of her shoes and walk across the wall-to-wall plush carpet, stroke the lace canopy over the bed, caress the velvet chair before the lace-draped vanity table and lean over to inhale the bouquet of white carnations and baby's breath in the silver vase on the bedside table.

''This is like something out of a fairy tale,'' she said at last.

Townsend shot him a pleased look before excusing himself and withdrawing. When the door closed behind him, Vincent asked, ''Now will you forgive me for kidnapping you?''

''One has nothing to do with the other,'' she replied with a touch of her previous asperity. Then her expression turned wistful. "Are the other rooms as wonderful as this?"

"No. In fact, most are closed away because I've no use for the space. Once you're feeling stronger you're welcome to explore, but be careful where you wander. Not every stairway or floor is as sound as it may seem."

"Once I'm stronger, I'll be returning home," she countered, her voice low but firm.

The answer wasn't unexpected and Vincent accepted it, content to stand there and absorb the picture she made. In her burgundy coat she looked like one of spring's first rosebuds rising out of a blanket of snow. The urge to pluck her close and satiate all the needs she stirred within him was one he had to make a conscious effort to resist. Did she know each cool pronouncement she made, each spirited rejection, was a thorn's slash against his heart that he suffered willingly, because the only other option—her silence or absence—was inconceivable? Deadly. Yes, he had it bad. Like an addict, he couldn't go on abusing himself this way; something would have to give. But he knew he had no desire to live without her, either.

"As you heard, dinner is at seven," he said at last. "If you find you're not up to coming downstairs..."

"I'll be there. I don't want my presence to cause Townsend more work than necessary."

"Ceara... as you wish. You might have noticed the double doors at the beginning of the hall. That's the elevator. It would please me if you'd use it."

"I'm not an invalid, nor a child who can't be trusted with stairs."

He watched her take out her deeper annoyance on her coat, ripping at the cloth belt and flinging the entire garment onto the bed. Beneath it she wore the dress he had purchased for her. Surprise and pleasure surged through him. He had expected never to see her in it again.

"No," he agreed thickly as he let his gaze caress her dancer's breasts, her slight waist, her slender hips. "But contrary to what you believe, you are very precious to me. If I can't spare your feelings, at least allow me to ensure your safety." Knowing if he stayed any longer, he would have to say, to do more, he spun on his heel and headed for the door.

"Vincent."

He paused, a hand on the knob.

"I'm not ungrateful. You've been . . . I do appreciate what you've done for me."

"I know you do," he replied, staring at the white enameled door. "As usual, your manners are impeccable. I only wish your heart was feeling more charitable."

He wasn't being fair, Ceara thought after resting and changing for dinner. Her expression was gloomy as she sat before the vanity mirror and tried to make each minute drag into two. If she was being hard-hearted, it was because he had made her so.

She grimaced at her appearance, deciding it wasn't helping her mood. There was no way she could arrange her hair to hide the bandage above her left temple; nor did her cinnamon suede jumpsuit's warm color offset the fact that she hadn't managed to get much rest. She was still pale, and that only emphasized the bruises on her face and her black eye.

"What difference does it make, anyway?" she muttered to herself. It wasn't as though she was out to impress Vincent, was she? Not quite able to meet her own eyes in the mirror, let alone answer that question, and accepting there wasn't much else she could do, she rose and began her journey downstairs for dinner.

At the top of the landing she considered the stairs. They didn't look all that difficult. But when she leaned over the balustrade and looked straight down to the foyer, dizziness overwhelmed her and she had to grip the railing and wait for the moment to pass. Perhaps it would be wiser to use the elevator.

The car whined and moaned in such protest on its slow journey down that when she reached for the ornamental sliding gate she wasn't at all surprised to see the wooden outer door open and find Vincent there to greet her. No, it was his appearance that, as usual, took her breath away.

Like her, he had changed. He was wearing a black silk shirt with black slacks. She was used to his penchant for surrounding himself with the color and found the full-sleeved shirt as individualistic as it was romantic. With his dark coloring, the grace with which he moved his powerful body, and with his courtly manners, he could have been a Renaissance lord.

"I hope the sound effects weren't disconcerting," he murmured, extending his hand to her.

Ceara would have preferred to avoid any physical contact with him, but a growing weakness in her limbs made that unavoidable. Placing her right hand in his, she replied, "Not really. It reminds me of the freight elevator at our company's distribution center. Am I late?" she added, growing less confident of her decision when he looped her arm around his, which forced her closer to his side.

"Townsend's only now lit the candles."

"He shouldn't be going to so much trouble." Through the silk of his shirt Ceara could feel Vincent's heat and his strength. In comparison her fingers felt damp, cool and unsteady. "I would have been content with a bowl of soup and a slice of sandwich in the kitchen."

"Why not a tray of bread and water shoved into your room through a door slot?" Vincent drawled.

"Now who's being overly dramatic? What I meant was that this is a huge place for one person to run alone."

"He periodically brings in help for seasonal cleaning, but otherwise he prefers solitude as much as I do."

Birds of a feather, Ceara mused, resisting the curiosity to ask how they had evolved this strange arrangement. She didn't need to know. The more she knew, the more she became involved herself.

They entered the dining room. Like the foyer, it was dark. The candelabra on the left side of the long table, where two place settings were laid out, did little to illuminate the rest of the room. What Ceara could see only reinforced her earlier impressions about stepping back in time. Red and gold were the dominant colors, appearing as brocade on the papered walls and matching floor-to-ceiling draperies. The table, long enough to comfortably seat twenty, was made of mahogany as was the buffet and china hutch. Oddly enough there were no paintings or ornamentation on the walls. How like Vincent, she thought, to ensure that those seated at his table wouldn't be distracted from their meals or each other. He was a man for whom concentration was a key that unlocked everything. But did he, in fact, ever entertain?

He led her to her chair and drew it out. Before she sat down she shot him a speaking glance that won her an unapologetic shrug.

"I simply thought we'd be able to hear each other better if we weren't sitting at opposite sides of the table."

Conversation wasn't something she was looking forward to. But knowing that this would at least make serving easier for Townsend, she bit back the dry response that came to mind.

Vincent took his own seat at the head of the table. "Were you able to get any sleep?"

For a moment Ceara could only stare. His face, illuminated by the flickering candlelight, took on a new mystery, all the angles becoming sharper, the lines deeper because they were cast in shadow. And his eyes appeared to be illuminated from within; golden flames beckoned like crooked fingers. She had to concentrate to answer. "No. But lying down helped."

"Perhaps some of this will, as well." Vincent reached for the opened wine bottle on his left. "It's had time to breathe. May I pour you some?"

"Only a little." Her blood was already racing too fast, too hot in her veins.

"Yes, you've always been interestingly indifferent to wine. This one you might find a worthy exception. It's not as heavy as some reds, and it's more fruity than nutty."

Ceara found herself tongue-tied, and that made her as frustrated as it did sad. Once she'd had no trouble finding things to talk about with Vincent. Every thought, every interest of his would have fascinated her, and she had once yearned to share everything with him. But now the very idea of having to hold up her end of a conversation was stressful. Their relationship had changed. He was part stranger—a charismatic one to be sure, but nevertheless one she wouldn't allow herself to respond to or trust.

He lifted his glass. "What shall we drink to?"

His low voice was a caress that sent ripples of awareness and excitement through her body. She had to stop this, stop him, she thought, barely able to hold her glass steady. "You're the creative one. Why don't you choose? Who knows? I might even drink enough of this so that I end up believing it."

And instead of waiting for him to respond, she sipped her wine because her throat was impossibly dry. She doubted she would be able to find her voice again, let alone swallow any food. Intensely aware of Vincent's silence, she was relieved when Townsend entered carrying two spinach salads on a silver tray. He set one before each of them and silently withdrew.

"He's very... reserved, isn't he?" she said, smoothening her linen napkin over her lap.

"Like you, he has a tendency to speak only when he has something to say."

Ceara's silverware chimed musically as she reached for and dropped her salad fork. She let her hand fall back into her lap. "This isn't going to work."

"Not if you're determined to lash out at me every time I speak to you." As soon as the words were out, Vincent shut his eyes and held up his hand. "All right. That wasn't fair, either." With a sigh he put down his own utensil. "I suspect I've no more of an appetite than you have, but we have to face the reality that neither our temperaments nor our constitutions will improve if we continue to deprive ourselves of nourishment. What do you say we try for five minutes of noncombative silence and give Townsend's efforts a fair chance?"

Because she didn't trust herself to reply, Ceara nodded and focused on her salad. Despite the sweetly tart dressing each bite tasted like wax, but she chewed until she could bring herself to swallow.

By the time Townsend carried in their main course, she had barely made more than a dent in the pretty greenery, but at least her hand had stopped shaking quite so badly. When she caught his discreet look, she cast him an apologetic smile to let him know she would try to do justice to the rest of the meal. As she expected, his expression remained stoic and sober, but something softened in his blue-gray eyes before he withdrew. A nice man, she decided. She would try to do better and not to hurt his feelings.

Ceara eyed the dessert Townsend placed before her and sighed inwardly. Caramel custard was one of the few treats that could tempt her barely existent sweet tooth, but she was pushing her luck. The portion of her dinner she had managed to eat lay like a rock in her stomach and another as a boulder in her throat. Only his attentiveness and his touching efforts to please kept her from refusing the treat outright. But as soon as he left the room, she broke the silence that had been lingering between her and Vincent to ask about something else that bothered her.

"Did you tell him to prepare this dessert in particular?"

"He inquired about your preferences. Do you mind?"

In a way she very much did, because it brought back painful memories of the last time she had helped Mrs. Green prepare it at her own home. That had been last Christmas Eve when Vincent joined them for an intimate dinner. The sweet-creamy flavors had lingered in her memory as she had walked him to the door where she had found the courage to alter what he had intended as an innocent good-night kiss on the cheek to an exciting but all-too-brief kiss on her lips. And while the kiss—not her first by any means—had touched her soul, it had also made her want and need as a woman. Oh, yes, she minded being forced to remember all that. The question was, did he remember or was this sheer coincidence?

With Vincent? Never.

She chose not to answer him and tried to concentrate on eating her dessert, but after only a taste, she had to put down her spoon. Her stomach rolled threateningly and her body grew hot and damp. She knew her reaction wasn't due to the few sips of wine she had indulged in. Her queasiness arose from her memories and the heartsickness over understanding how all her caring and dreams had been a waste.

Pushing back her chair, she dragged her crushed napkin from her lap and set it on the table. "I don't think I can . . . excuse me."

Somehow she got to her feet and made it out of the room. Blindly, and thinking only of the sanctuary her bed would provide, Ceara crossed the foyer and started up the stairs. By the time she was a third of the way up, she realized her mistake. Vertigo struck. If it wasn't for Vincent's strong hands gripping her waist, she knew she would have lost her balance.

"Little fool," he growled, drawing her back against the rock-hard steadiness of his body. "Do you loathe every memory of me so much you're willing to kill yourself to obliterate them?"

Dazed, she shook her head. "I didn't think about the stairs when..." The room wouldn't stop spinning. Succumbing to it, Ceara rested her head back against him. Just for a moment, she assured herself, until the worst passed. Only she soon realized that what replaced the dizziness was far more dangerous.

Vincent's chest rose and fell with every deep, controlled breath he drew in. She could feel the powerful beat of his heart against her back and the gentle caress of his hands. He began soothing her, drawing slow circles with this thumbs around the small of her back. Each stroke sensitized and warmed the most secret parts of her.

"I know what you're thinking. Neither of us can help it," he whispered near her ear. "I was remembering that night, too."

"Don't. I don't want to think about it."

"And I can't stop. It was the beginning of the end for me. I realize that now. No matter what I'd promised Carson, that night I touched you the way a man touches a woman...and all those walls of defense I'd been building started trembling at their foundations."

"Words."

"Truth."

He spun her around. Because he stood on a lower stair, she found herself almost at eye level with him. She had to shut her lids to keep from becoming hypnotized by the power he exuded.

"The truth," he repeated, his voice gaining an edge she was unfamiliar with. "That one reckless kiss tasted of sweetness and innocence and dreams. Do you know how I wished...*wish* I could turn back the years to where I could match you your innocence and pure spirit? But it was *too late,*" he groaned, touching his lips to her forehead.

How was it possible to feel your heart break twice over the same man? Ceara wondered, barely able to breathe through the pain memory and his closeness brought. She curled her hands into fists. "Innocence?" she whispered shakily, determined not to let him do this to her ever again. "I may have been then, but what makes you think I am now?"

His head jerked back as though struck; his gaze burned into her. "Don't make jokes," he warned.

She could hear the voice in the back of her mind asking her what lunacy she thought she was toying with, but she ignored it. "I wouldn't think of it," she drawled, for the first time wishing she were a more gifted actress. "Besides, if there is a joke, it's on me for once believing it was important to save yourself for one man, the man you loved."

"You still believe that."

"Do I?"

"I know you, Ceara."

She laughed, but the sound was closer to a sob. "You know and see what you want."

"No."

His face turned gray, and the skin stretched over his high cheekbones grew impossibly taut. Before she knew it he slipped one strong arm around her and brought her completely against his body, closer than they had ever been before.

"Do you know what I'd do to the man who ever dared touch you?" he growled, his breath hot against her lips. "Say it isn't true. *Say it.*"

The grip of his hands biting into her waist and closing around the back of her neck was painful, but it was a pain she welcomed. She doubted anything else would have kept her from dropping in a dead faint. Never had she heard him say anything so outrageously possessive or sound this angry.

"It's not true," she managed to reply.

He lowered his gaze, for the first time realizing the fierce hold he had on her. His expression changed to one of despair and self-loathing. With a muffled groan he released her. "Why?" he rasped. "Why torment us both like this?"

Ceara gripped the banister to keep from sinking to the carpeted steps. "Because . . . I wanted to hurt you. Because I wanted you to experience the same pain you've been causing me."

All the fire and passion died in his eyes.

"Shocking, isn't it?" she added, although her throat felt raw. "But then why should it be? You've been an excellent tutor, Vincent."

He took a step backward, descending a stair as though he had taken a blow to his chest. His face, his entire being was that of a man facing reality for the first time and finding it unbearable.

Ceara, too, had endured enough. Wanting only to escape to her room, she turned, and it was then that she spotted Townsend standing just inside the doorway of the dining room. It was his black suit that had allowed him to blend in with the shadows, his silence that had made him a witness. An unwelcome witness, she thought with an instant of distress and humiliation.

But it hadn't been his intention to eavesdrop, she realized in the next moment. Vincent's words from the other day drifted back through her memory. Yes, she could see by a certain something in his eyes that Townsend had stayed near in case she had needed protecting from the employer he devoted himself to.

What would he say, she wondered, if she told him that what she really needed was protection from herself?

Shaking her head sadly, apologetically, she drew on what was left of her strength and completed her journey up the stairs.

Chapter Five

For two full days Ceara kept to her room and Vincent stalked through the house like a convict pacing the length and width of his cell, listening for a sound that might mean a reprieve.

None came.

Every few hours he climbed the stairs, went to her door and listened. But all remained silent.

Townsend approached him with similar regularity, inquiring whether he would take a meal. He sent him away, sometimes by ignoring him, sometimes with a wave of his hand, occasionally with an oath; however, he always called him back and asked him to go upstairs and find out if Ceara needed anything, only to discover she was far more eloquent in her silence than he could hope to be.

He didn't know what to do. In the past he had managed to get through the stressful, troubled periods of his life by throwing himself into his work. He let his stories devour his surplus energy; he bequeathed his passion and frustrations to his characters. Now even they were abandoning him, keeping to the farthermost recesses of his mind, shunning him as though he were the most hideous of beings, not even worthy of their transitory presence.

He was dying. Grief and loneliness were slowly annihilating him. Time was torture. With each passing hour he could feel himself being consumed from the inside out. How long, how long before his shell caved in on the widening emptiness?

On the morning of the third day he received a call. Few people had his unlisted number, which undoubtedly meant it was someone he would normally care to speak to, yet he remained indifferent, slumped in the leather armchair in his study, a long stride away from the desk extension. Midway through the sixth or seventh ring it stopped. Not a moment too soon, Vincent thought, ready to take the whole contraption and send it through the bay window behind his desk. Shortly afterward Townsend appeared in the doorway.

"That was your editor."

"I'm not taking calls."

"He's aware of that. He was inquiring as to when the status might change?"

"It's not," Vincent growled. Then he sighed. "Have you been upstairs recently?"

"An hour ago. There's nothing new to report."

He felt another nail secure the lid on his coffin. "If she doesn't come down by noon, I'm going to break the blasted door down. This is the third day, damn it! It's unnatural for her to go without nourishment for this long."

"She has a bowl of fruit in there. In any case, there's been many a time you've done as much yourself when you're working."

"I haven't just been released from a hospital. She'll make herself ill again. For all we know she's up there unconscious."

As it had for days now, his panic fed on itself and mushroomed. Vincent dragged himself to his feet, rubbing his hands over his bewhiskered face and through his unkempt hair. He hadn't shaved or changed his clothes since their catastrophic dinner and he knew he must look like a nightmare character out of a Poe novel. He needed to pull himself together, go upstairs and get cleaned up in case Ceara came down. It would only add to her uneasiness to find him looking like this.

What makes you think she plans to come down?

"I need a drink," he muttered, crossing to the brandy decanter that was almost empty.

"I doubt your liver agrees," Townsend drawled.

"My liver can go to hell with the rest of me. Now go away."

Townsend obliged him, but Vincent didn't pour the brandy, after all. Instead he dropped back into his chair and, resting his elbows on his knees, buried his face in his hands.

He wasn't sure how long he stayed like that or if, perhaps, exhaustion didn't momentarily overcome him. But something—a presence, filtered into his consciousness. He raised his head . . . and there she was.

She stood like a statue at the base of the stairs, looking frail but lovely in an emerald-green sweater and slacks. He could tell by the way she gripped the banister that she didn't want this confrontation, but was resigning herself to the inevitability of it.

"So you've come out at last," he said, his throat raw from drink and fatigue.

"Yes."

"Yes. There's a stingy soliloquy. A bird is more communicative. And she stands there so unsure and wary," he muttered aside, although his heart wrenched anew for the misery he had brought her. "Relax, fair Ceara," he added, his voice and ire growing stronger. "You have my word that I won't pounce. The Beast is tethered and Beauty is safe."

"You've been drinking."

"Not since dawn."

She shook her head. "You always start sounding like an English stage actor when you drink."

"Why not, since my life seems to be unfolding like a Shakespearean tragedy—or am I confusing his comedies with his tragedies?" When she failed to respond, he intoned, "That was my best attempt at humor, my dear. Believe me, it goes downhill from here."

Ceara drew a deep breath and came down the rest of the stairs, crossed the foyer and paused just inside the study's doorway. "When was the last time you ate?"

"When did you?"

"I'm about to do something about my condition. You, on the other hand, look as though you're determined to run yourself into the ground."

He picked up the empty glass on the table beside him and saluted her with it. "Here's to the greater resiliency of youth."

"Self-pity doesn't become you, Vincent."

His laugh was hard and brief, and he set down the glass with such force that the table rocked. "My God, I underestimated you. Since Monday night, you've cloistered yourself away like a little nun. I drove myself half-mad with worry over your silent grieving. Anything, I thought, anything would be better than this, and I willed you to come down and unleash your worst. I could have withstood—no, *welcomed* your fury, even your tears." He gestured with a dramatic sweep of his arm. "Yet there you stand, dry-eyed, pale to be sure, but with your mouth pinched, not trembling, with pent-up emotion."

"The time for tears is past."

Her voice was quiet and calm, and he went cold at the thought of what new resolve she was embracing. "So you've healed yourself." He glanced away. "A part of me can't help but be grateful for that no matter how it came about. However," he added more bitterly, swinging his gaze back to her, "you'll understand if another part remains less than euphoric with your censure of me because I've failed to achieve what you have."

"I'm disappointed that you should be so willing to find oblivion inside a bottle."

"I *seek* oblivion," he corrected. "But, as you can see, we haven't yet made each other's acquaintance."

"Vincent . . . it's time to move on."

"Can you?"

"I have to."

"So much for all those feelings you claimed to hold for me. I contend this proves they weren't as deep as you purported. Well, why should they have been?" he drawled, miring deeper in his bitterness. "You're young. You have a lifetime of experience to collect before you can have a basis for comparison. *I*, on the other hand, have an acute and clear understanding of what I've glimpsed and lost. In other words, my dear, kindly allow me to mourn its passing in my own way."

"There you go again with those elusive references to your past," Ceara cried, lifting her hands, palms upward. "How can I understand any of this if I don't know what you're talking about? Haven't I earned a right to know?"

Suddenly feeling the full weight of his age, as well as his fatigue, Vincent closed his eyes. "Of all the things you could ask for—never mind. You shall have your lodestone. Come in and sit down. At least be comfortable while I finish shattering the remaining illusions you have of me."

Ceara looked as though she might resist, but then quickly crossed the room, choosing the navy-and-green-striped couch he occasionally used when exhaustion claimed him after an around-the-clock bout at the computer. The pillow she took and hugged to her breasts was the one on which he would rest his head. Envious of the inanimate object, he rose and stepped behind his chair, wishing he could put even more distance between them.

"As you already know, I attended a small college in Massachusetts," he began. "What I never explained was that I didn't graduate. I was asked to leave early in my final year... by my father." He paused and glanced at Ceara, drinking in her youth and beauty. How would she look at him when he completed his story? he wondered. "As you also know, he was the head of the English Department, and I'd originally chosen Demarest because it was his school. Though he was a demanding teacher and father, I...I loved and respected him a great deal.

"My first three years passed well enough. My father was disappointed that I wasn't turning out to be the scholar he'd hoped for, but I was finding my niche as a writer for the school paper. That placated him somewhat. If he couldn't have another academic in the family, he reasoned, perhaps a Pulitzer prizewinning writer would be the next best thing. Don't you suppose he's spinning in his grave now?''

"Your novels are wonderful," Ceara said, a frown marring her brow. "They're smoothly written, fast-paced, thought-provoking..."

"And above all marketable," Vincent injected dryly, then shrugged, dismissing the subject. "But I digress. Over the summer, just before my senior year, an old friend of my father's joined the staff. He was a bookish, sensitive man who'd come from one of the larger universities. My father explained that politics and pressure had affected his health. His friend wanted a quieter life for himself and his new—bride."

"Was this his first marriage?" Ceara shrugged when he shot her a questioning look. "If he was a friend of your father's...he just sounded old enough to have been married more than once."

"Yes, he and my father were close in age and, no, he'd never been married before. Eric was...painfully shy." Vincent shook his head and laughed bitterly. "Renee wasn't. She was young and as ambitious as she was sensual. By marrying Eric, she thought she'd found a shortcut to a higher social circle. Only she didn't know how tedious life could be on a small campus."

Ceara bowed her head. "You...you had an affair with her."

"She chose me to keep boredom at bay, and I was too flattered, too eager to care about anything but relieving my own sexual frustrations. You want to call it an 'affair,' Ceara? I was too shallow and single-minded to do the word justice. What harm was I causing? I asked myself. Surely by now Eric knew what she was? Even if he didn't, I believed we were being discreet enough so that neither he nor anyone else would find out. But I was wrong. He did find out. Everyone did."

"She told him."

"Yes...she told him. One night, having decided she'd endured enough, she entertained him with a detailed account of our...trysts."

Ceara bowed her head. "What a horrible woman."

"One can only imagine what kind of lout would succumb to her lure, eh?"

She looked up again, a spasm of pain crossing her face. "Finish your story. No doubt her husband was hurt?"

"Such delicate phrasing. Do you know what he did? He went out to the backyard with the shotgun she'd bought him for duck hunting and he killed himself. Can you see the irony of it? Even knowing what she'd done to him, he was considerate about *inconveniencing* her."

Ceara pressed a hand to her mouth and closed her eyes. Vincent knew that had she been able to she would have covered her ears, as well.

"Look at me," he challenged. "You see before you a man who not only committed the ultimate sin, but destroyed a friendship—and why? Because of love? No. *Lust.*" He drew a deep breath. "Are you beginning to understand? This isn't something I've ever been able to turn my back on. My father disowned me and ordered me out of his house. For years I was considered persona non grata in the very home I grew up in. When he and my mother died six years ago in that hotel fire in Europe, I still didn't know if he'd ever forgiven me."

Ceara remained silent. Incredulous, afraid he understood only too well why, Vincent backed a step away from her and taunted, "She resists adding her denunciation to the others' and then wonders why she enchanted me. Ceara, *Ceara*, you see before you a monster and you don't recoil in revulsion?"

"You're not a monster, Vincent."

"No, because even a monster is pitiable in that he's another's creation, therefore helpless to change himself. I know. I *chose*. No one could despise me more than I despised myself, and that was why I began withdrawing from the world. Writing helped me achieve the seclusion I craved and knew I deserved. Isn't it ironic that fate should reward me with success in order that I might carry out my own sentence?"

"Have you considered the possibility that you're misinterpreting its message? Perhaps it's trying to tell you that it's time to put your past behind you."

"I thought so, too... for a while, especially when I met your father. Carson was decent and intelligent and he reminded me of the father I no longer had, the friend I'd long been denying myself. Can you imagine how humbled I was when he invited me to his home? Against my better judgment, inwardly terrified that a tattoo announcing my unworthiness would appear stamped on my forehead exposing me, I went. And there you were."

Ceara rose, took a step and stopped, as if not knowing what to do.

"You were like dawn after an interminable night," he continued, remembering. "So new and vibrant and untouched by life's ugliness. When we both stooped to snatch up your fallen scarf, your fingers brushed mine. That's all... a forgettable occurrence happening between dozens of people every day. Only I didn't forget because that brief contact went through me like white heat. It pierced a heart I'd believed was frozen and brought me back to life. Even the pain of it was exquisite.''

"You were so moved you refused our next three invitations," Ceara reminded him, continuing to clutch the sofa pillow to her.

"Of course I did. I told you, I was terrified of exposing myself... and of what you stirred in me when we were together.''

He tried to gauge her feelings by her expression. But all he could see mirrored was grief and... what? Disappointment. In him, naturally, for no one else deserved it. But surely she had more to say. If she despised him for his weakness and selfishness, then he wanted to hear it. Now. If she could understand and forgive...

"When we first met, I thought you were the most gallant, mysterious man I'd ever met," she said, her face turned toward the foyer but her eyes vague and focused on some inward scene. "I'd heard all the stories going around about you, so you were already larger than life in my mind. Our meeting enhanced that. And yet... I saw something else in you that I didn't think too many others had noticed. You had a tender spirit.''

"What you saw was only a reflection of a greater tenderness. Yours, Ceara." He stepped toward her. "Now do you understand how easy it was to promise your father that his only child would be safe from me? You deserved a whole man who wouldn't cringe at the very thought of appearing in public, a good man whose past is as unsullied as yours. As much as I... It was impossible. Wrong. *Do* you see?''

Ceara gave him a brief shake of her head before lifting her chin and meeting his gaze. "Only that you think I should be passed on to some product of incubation like myself. I'm sorry, Vincent. All I see is a man who didn't atone but was defeated by his mistakes. What you did was terrible, yes, and something that you'll always have to live with. But you chose the easier method of dealing with it. You withdrew from a world that might criticize you. And you withdrew from me, hiding behind the pretense of caring too much."

"It wasn't pretense!"

"It was!" she cried back. "It would have taken a greater courage to live up to your feelings, not turn your back on them. There lies your shame, Vincent, and as a result of it—and only that one—do I reject this explanation and you, because I am more honest. Because I did dare."

As if suddenly snapping out of a trance, her expression grew momentarily horrified. Then she flung away the pillow and bolted for the door. Pained though he was by her criticism, Vincent knew she was right, just as he knew he couldn't let her go.

"Wait!" He grabbed her wrist, but gently so as not to upset her any more than she already was. "We'll try again."

Her answering look was incredulous and she shook her head. "That's impossible. We can never go back to what we were. We've hurt each other too much."

"I'll spend the rest of my life making up for the hurt I've caused you."

"I don't want your penance, any more than you would accept my pity."

"No?" As she tried to free herself from his grasp, he adjusted his hold to frame her face with his hands. "At this point I'm desperate enough to take what I can get from you. Ceara. We could be happy here."

"Then you'd be doing us both an injustice." She stifled a soft moan by compressing her lips. "Oh, Vincent . . . we're not modern people, you and I. You through your trials and I through being brought up in an overly protected environment that allowed only a homogenized version of life to filter through—we're stuck respecting old values, honoring personal principle. Those things mean *everything* to us. And so you could no more ask me to join you in your personal purgatory, because that's what this place has become for you—not reclusiveness for an ideal as some have sought it, but a private purging ground—than I could stay knowing that. You would be asking me to abandon my own sense of self-worth and live in guilt as you are.''

"All I know is that I'm not ready to let you walk out of my life.''

"I believe you mean that, but those aren't words born of a positive rejuvenating kind of caring.''

"They are,'' he insisted, enfolding her close. "Ceara, can't you feel it?'' He pressed a kiss to one of her temples and then the other. Having stored his passion for years, he felt like a great mountain shuddering from within, about to erupt with too-long contained feelings. Here within his hands he held his light, his sun. How could she doubt he wouldn't be rejuvenated by her? With only one kiss she could make his soul soar with the angels. Seeking it, he brushed her lips against hers, coaxing her to respond.

Instead she stiffened.

He raised his head and searched her lovely but resolute face. "Kiss me, Ceara,'' he whispered, caressing her cheek with his thumb.

"No.''

"You want to. Look at me. I know I'll see it in your eyes.''

"I can't help what you see there, but I also know it would be a mistake to give in to it."

Such rational words from one small woman who was trembling as much as he was. He knew he would only have to kiss her with a portion of the desire churning within him and she would forget her protestations and be his. His body throbbed at the very thought of finally having what he had long yearned to cherish.

Yet in a way she was right—but only that his timing was off. It would be a mistake to push any harder now. He had overwhelmed her with information and shown her a side of himself that was hardly commendable. She needed time to sort through it all.

With a deep and not unpainful breath he nodded, exhaled and offered her an unsteady but reassuring smile. "You see how good you are for me? Your calm, strong will reaches through my impatience and reasons with my selfishness."

"Vincent . . ."

"Come. We've punished ourselves enough. We need food and then sleep. Let's go to the kitchen and give Townsend a shock. All this time he's expected to have to tackle me to keep me from charging upstairs and breaking down your door. He's liable to drop his dentures when he sees us walk in arm in arm, demanding food."

As he tried to link his arm through hers, Ceara held him off. "You're frightening me. Haven't you listened to a word I've said?"

"Every one."

"No. You've said your piece and now you think everything is washed clean as though it never existed."

With a firm shake of his head Vincent lifted her chin to meet his grave look. "Not clean. Never everything.

I'm too much a realist to try to convince myself of that. But I also know that you could no more turn your back on me than I could walk away from you. Our souls are linked by something greater than we are, Ceara . . . and so for the moment I'm content to leave our destinies to providence. Right now I'll settle for focusing on feeding you. Come."

Grasping her hand, he lifted it to his lips for an impassioned kiss. Then, with a look that was as possessive as it was determined, he led her toward the kitchen.

It was just over an hour later that Ceara managed to return to her room. She felt less hungry than before—because she had managed to eat a little—but she was more troubled than ever. Heading straight to the window bench seat, she curled among the velvet and lace pillows arranged there.

Outside the sky was stormy again, the clouds heavy with the promise of rain. The wind blew in gusts, tearing at the dying leaves, ripping many from their gnarled branches. Nature's mood was no less tortured than her own.

Vincent wasn't going to let her go quietly. She leaned her head against the cool windowpane and accepted the wrenching hurt that came with the knowledge and from the battle her mind had already waged with her heart. What was she going to do?

His story had struck her yet another devastating blow. It wasn't because she was naive; she knew situations like his happened, unfortunately, all too often in this day and age. Only they weren't supposed to happen to people she knew. They weren't supposed to involve *Vincent*. That hurt most. She had held him in such high esteem.

No, she couldn't deny she was crushed by what he had done, just as she couldn't deny she remained desperately in love with him. But that love would turn destructive if she didn't put some distance between them, and soon. Things were already changing; she could feel it inside herself.

She had to get away before he assumed too much control over her life. Hindsight allowed her to recognize the inevitability of that; the pattern she saw evolving wasn't all that dissimilar to the way her father had manipulated her. But at least her father had been protecting his child, the last flesh and blood connection he'd had with his own soul mate, her mother. Put in that perspective, it was easier to forgive him his emotional tug-of-war. Vincent's behavior could easily go beyond that; he could become obsessive. While a part of her thrilled to bask in the romantic fantasy of being wanted so much, common sense forced her to admit it wouldn't be a healthy situation for either of them. There would no independence for her; there would be no equality in their relationship. Never again would she give her heart to a man who saw her more as a treasure to be tucked away than a partner. That kind of loving could only suffocate her. The tragedy was that Vincent couldn't see that it was all he was offering her.

Oh, she was miserable. As miserable as when she had loved and believed those feelings weren't returned. "Help me," she moaned, hugging her forehead to her knees. "Oh, God, help me to know what to do."

Chapter Six

Somehow a week passed. Ceara found it helped to let Townsend and Vincent insist she get more bed rest, and she actually managed to sleep several extra hours a day, which allowed her to avoid having any further confrontations with Vincent such as the one they'd had in his study. But even his periodical visits to her room were stressful. For her. *He* seemed rejuvenated, as though a great weight had been lifted off him, and he became almost cheerful.

On Monday, ten days after her accident, Ceara came out of the bathroom from a shower to find Townsend had delivered her breakfast tray and was drawing the sheers back from the windows along with the heavy draperies, the way she liked it. Sunbeams shot into the room and bounced off the walls, carpet, everything, and stung her eyes as though they were reflecting off snow.

"Oh, it's going to be a lovely day," she sighed, at once pleased yet wistful.

Townsend offered her his usual ceremonial bow.
"Good morning, miss. Where would you prefer to be
served?"

"The window bench?" Ceara asked, self-consciously
adjusting the collar of her white bathrobe, even though
the lush terry cloth covered her from neck to ankle. "I'd
like to watch the birds and squirrels this morning."

"Very well, but you won't let yourself get chilled with
that damp hair, will you?"

Ceara was impressed. As usual, he had barely spared
her a glance, and yet she had a feeling there was little
that he missed. "I promise." She fingered the fresh
bandage she had put on after her careful shower.
"Townsend...do you know of a doctor in town? It's
been ten days, and I'm sure these stitches can be removed, but I'd hate to bother Mr. Dante to take me
back to the city when he's working. He is working, isn't
he?"

"He is, indeed. For hours now. However, I'm sure he
wouldn't mind—"

"No...no. He's wasted too much time on my problems already. Let him be."

"In that case there's a fine general practitioner in
Mapleton, miss. Shall I call when I return downstairs?
I'm sure he could make arrangements to see you."

Ceara thanked him and he excused himself. He returned a half hour later to collect the tray and advised
her that the doctor agreed to see her whenever she could
get into town.

"I'm prepared to drive you whenever you care to
leave," he added.

The prospect of once again being escorted and
watched over as she had been this past week was more
than she could bear, and Ceara bit her lip, wondering

how to go about explaining as much without hurting his feelings or causing an affront to his professional pride. "Townsend, may I be frank?"

"I would hope you always feel free to be so, miss."

"Then do you mind if I borrow a car and go by myself? Mr. Dante does have more than one, doesn't he?"

"Most certainly. Besides the sedan there's a four-wheel-drive vehicle for when the weather gets severe. But you're barely back on your feet and it's more than a half-hour drive to town. Mr. Dante..."

"Wouldn't need to know. I won't be gone long, and as you said, he's working," she gushed eagerly. "I'll be back before he misses me."

Ever the gentleman, Townsend ducked his head and straightened his tie. "May *I* speak frankly, Miss Lowell?"

"Fair's fair... if you'll call me Ceara."

"Thank you, Miss Ceara. In that case, may I remind you how Mr. Dante is—oh, dear, how shall I put this delicately?—extremely sensitive to your well-being. It would be a serious underestimation on your part to assume that because he's closed himself in his study he isn't... er, attuned to your whereabouts."

"Then you have to help me, Townsend."

"I was afraid you were going to say something like that, miss."

An hour later, despite worrying that Vincent would indeed catch her in the act, Ceara managed to slip out the back of the house and drive off in the sedan. She held her breath until she passed through the front gates, which Townsend electronically opened for her, and indulged in a great sigh of relief, and the closest thing to a lighthearted chuckle she had managed in weeks.

She wasn't exactly comfortable driving an unfamiliar vehicle, but what she lacked in confidence she made up for with excitement. For the first time since her accident she was truly free, the autumn day was sparkling like a jeweled brooch and she was going to get her annoying, ugly stitches out. What more could she ask for? she wondered of the twinkling-eyed woman reflected in the rearview mirror.

Her bruises were fading fast and makeup had helped mute the lingering discoloration. Except for the bandage, she looked almost like her old self, and *that* meant once she spoke with the doctor and made sure everything was all right, she had a major confrontation to look forward to. She had to tell Vincent it was time for her to leave. That was another reason why she wanted a few hours out, alone. She needed to build up the courage to say goodbye. Would it be possible, even with all the tension and heartache between them? She wasn't feeling as confident as she knew she needed to be, but one thing she did know—a parting was necessary.

"What have I done?"

Ceara stared at herself in the mirror that ran the length of the hair salon. It had been sheer impulse. She had left the doctor's office, feeling as though everyone were staring at the gaping bare spot above her temple. And the next thing she knew she was standing before the front door of this place, reading the sign that said, Walk-ins Welcome.

Now her eighteen-inch-long tresses were lying in a semicircle at the base of her chair. What remained of her ash-brown hair was as short as a boy's. Actually, she had seen plenty of youths with longer hair.

"It's a shock, I know," the grinning stylist said, bending so that their reflections met cheek to cheek. "I was no different when I got mine cut off, and it'd been long enough to sit on."

Aghast, Ceara met the slim blonde's eyes in the mirror. "How did you ... you look wonderful, but ... how could you bear it?"

The young woman who had introduced herself as G.G. fussed a bit more with Ceara's spiky sideburns and replied, "I wasn't thinking with a clear head. I'd just broken up with my boyfriend and I did it to prove we were through. See, he was totally neurotic about my hair. It was my way of saying, 'So long, chum.'"

Is that what she had done? Ceara refocused on her reflection. Was she so much a coward that she had been looking for a way to drive a message home to Vincent that he would understand?

"Trust me, you look like a million bucks. With my face the best I can achieve is a strong resemblance to Tinkerbell's second cousin, but on you it's very chic and sophisticated. Keep it swept to that side and your bangs will cover the wound. Once that spot grows out, you can alternate partings or brush it forward for a more artsy look."

Ceara hardly heard the last part because she was concentrating on G.G.'s previous comment. *Chic? Sophisticated?* The style did seem to define her bone structure. Then again, unless she wore the right makeup, she was going to look like an eleven-year-old boy. She could experiment once she was back in the car. The style really did give her a certain feeling of confidence and zest.

"I think it'll grow on me," she murmured.

She paid and tipped the stylist and left the shop, returning to her car where she reapplied her lipstick, using a shade darker color, and added a touch of eyeliner, something that until now she rarely bothered with except for evening engagements. The transformation after those subtle alterations brought a bright smile to her face.

Earrings, she thought, turning her head side to side. Before she hadn't bothered with them, either, but now her ears showed. Something in gold would be nice. Maybe hoops? She shifted in her seat to scan the stores bordering this side of the charming park nestled in the center of town. There didn't seem to be a jewelry store among them, but no doubt if she drove around the square she would find one. Mapleton wasn't what she would call a city or even a large town; it was more of a village. But she loved the New England flavor of the place, the whitewashed or bricked, shuttered-windowed offices, the stores where rather than modern glass fronts there were multipaned, wood-bordered display windows. The sidewalks were quaint, too; cobblestones with lovely planters bordering the street. Each pot was filled with a thriving maple tree and adorned at its base with marigolds.

Ceara eased out of the parking slot and drove around the park, noting something else she found delightful about the place. Although there were some people who dressed casually, by and large the men were in suits and the women wore dresses. Several older ladies even wore hats and gloves. One matronly pair strolled in front of a pale-yellow-and-white two-storied house that Ceara realized was a bed-and-breakfast establishment. Beside it on the left she spotted the jewelry store she had been hoping to find. It was the building on the right of the bed-and-breakfast, however, that had her steering eagerly into the first empty parking slot she found. The stone house looked straight out of a fairy tale. The modest sign out front indicated that it was a new-and-used bookstore, which convinced Ceara all the more that she couldn't resist going inside to look around once she finished her other shopping. If there was one place she had never been able to resist, it was a bookstore.

Nearly a half hour later she emerged from the jeweler's carrying a bag containing two pairs of earring. She lifted a hand to her newly pierced ears. This was, she decided, fingering the delicate gold hoops, a day for firsts. Up until today she had never been tempted to pierce her ears, but the selections for post earrings had been so much nicer than the clip-on variety that she couldn't resist. No doubt her earlobes were going to stay as red as cherries and feel as huge as an elephant's for a while, but otherwise she felt blissfully happy with her minor adventure.

Tucking her small sack into her purse, she walked down the cobblestone sidewalk to the bookstore. Like the Lemon Tree Bed and Breakfast, it had a fenced front yard; in this case wrought iron compared to the Lemon Tree's white picket. The yards were connected by an iron gate and both areas had been transformed into a maze of flower beds and walkways. From the lingering greenery it appeared that in the height of blooming season every variety of flower was represented there. Now, however, there were mostly a few sturdy marigolds, and fall's most grateful flower, the chrysanthemum.

In the middle of one of the beds was a handmade sign reading For Sale, but anyone would have missed it unless they were intentionally searching for it. Its half-hearted appearance brought a whimsical smile to her lips, and Ceara climbed the stone steps and entered the building.

A tiny brass bell jingled cheerfully. It brought a huge yellowish-gray Persian cat from around a corner, which came over to rub against her legs in greeting. Ceara laughed softly and bent to scratch him behind his ears; it had to be a *he,* she decided, because she had never seen a feline larger that wasn't caged.

"Hello. I take it you're the host and security guard?"

She received a low purr in reply and the cat wandered off, leaving her to inspect her surroundings on her own. The entryway opened to what originally must have been a living room. Now the area was arranged for browsing through new and upcoming releases and for checking out purchases. Cozy upholstered chairs and a love seat were tucked back against the plants lining the large bay window. A cashier's counter took up another side of the room.

"Anyone here?" Ceara called, wandering to the next room, and then the next. She loved the way each was set up for a different genre. At the same time she imagined what she would change if this were hers. More chairs to encourage people to stay and browse in convenience, she mused. And more plants to continue the warm, friendly atmosphere she sensed in the front room. Of course, the place needed a good cleaning; also, while the floral wallpaper was perfect for the historical romance room, all the rest needed stripping and a new coat of paint.

"We're not open."

Ceara spun around, pressing a hand against the maroon-and-black scarf she'd secured like a necktie around her white tailored blouse. "You're not?" She stared at the short, wizened man who gave her a blue-frost glare from beneath two white bushy eyebrows. "Oh, I'm ... disappointed. You see, I fell in love with your store the moment I spotted it."

His short red nose wrinkled, causing his eyes to all but disappear. "Well...we're not officially closed," he amended. Then he added more forcefully, "I just don't have time to mess with the place. Got too many things to do as it is."

"Caring for the grounds, you mean," Ceara said, guessing by his clothing as much as his gnarled, weathered hands. "You do beautiful work."

He looked surprised, then pleased. Finally he shrugged away her compliment. "Most of the best blooms were done in by last week's frost. Gotta clean 'em out. Course, I don't know what I'll be putting in their place. Don't see how it'll make sense to put up the Christmas decorations the way I used to."

"Has the store been sold?" Ceara asked, unable to explain a sudden rush of disappointment.

"Er, no. But it might. Who knows? Then where would I be? Just have to take the whole mess down again."

"Aha." Ceara loved his grumble-bear personality. "So this is your store?"

"Guess so. Now. Was me an' my sister's, but Naomi passed on a couple of months ago." He drew a deep breath and glanced around, looking as irritated as he did sad. "What do I know about books? Naomi was the educated one in the family. Sharp, too. Knew where anything was that you might want." He glanced at Ceara. "Guess I could write you up a receipt if you happened to find something you wanted, though."

"I appreciate that. What I think I really want to know is...how was business? I mean, when your sister ran the place?"

"That's a nosy question to be asking a person."

"I know. But—" she bit her lip and shrugged "—would you believe I think I'm interested in the place?"

Immediately the old man's brow unfurled. "Why didn't you say so? I have to admit I saw you as one of those salespeople selling advertisements in the county paper or something. Well, let me start from the beginning," he said, rubbing his hand against the front of his shirt, but never actually offering it to her. "The name's Boone. Boone Tolliver, ma'am, and I'm pleasured to make your acquaintanceship. Now about the business—it kept us comfortable, you know what I mean? Naomi and the ladies next door had a thing going. They'd supply the tea and cakes and Naomi would have monthly readings. For the big holidays they'd do something for the kids. Halloween I had my work cut out for me. Christmas, too. I put my foot down at Easter, though. No way Naomi was going to get me into a rabbit suit."

Ceara nodded and pretended to search her purse for her small notebook and a pen in order to hide a grin. What a darling, she thought, and what a handful he would be if she could get him to stay on. "What's upstairs?" she asked when he paused to catch his breath.

"Our rooms."

"May I see them?"

"Sure, but watch yourself on the steps. That dang cat might trip you if'n he gets half a chance. Scram, Moss."

"Moss?"

"Naomi visited a friend down in Georgia once. Said that cat is the same color of that Spanish stuff hanging from their trees. Sometimes I think Naomi kinda overdosed on books, know what I mean?"

"What do you mean she took the car to Mapleton?" Vincent demanded of Townsend. "Why didn't you drive her?"

"She preferred being alone."

"She's been alone most of every day for the past week," Vincent said, summarily disqualifying the explanation. "When did she leave? How long has she been gone?"

"Since nearly ten this morning."

Vincent couldn't believe what he was hearing. Now he wished he had listened this morning when an inner voice had whispered that he should seek her out. "But it's past four! It'll be dark in another hour. When were you planning on telling me she was missing?"

"We don't know she is, sir."

"She could have had another accident or be lost. Good Lord, you know she wasn't in any condition to drive anywhere."

"On the contrary, she assured me she felt splendid, and that she would take the utmost care."

She would promise anything to get away from here, Vincent brooded, growing more concerned by the moment. If he'd had his suspicions before, he was certain now. No wonder Ceara had been so agreeable all week, staying in her room, pretending to get rest. What doctor's visit could have taken this long? Would she have dared to drive all the way back to New York? It wasn't unfeasible. She could always have someone from the office return his car. What a fool he had been to assure himself that she was getting used to the idea of being here with him, to believe she had begun to forgive him . . . want him, as he knew she once did.

"Call the police," he ordered, raking his hand through his hair. "Then bring the other car around front. I'll go get my coat and . . ."

The front gate's security buzzer sounded in his study. Suddenly reminded that there was a matching one in the kitchen, and realizing how Ceara had escaped without his knowledge, Vincent shot Townsend a rancorous look. Not only had the traitor condoned Ceara's slipping away, but he was behind her getting out the front gates this morning.

He stalked to his desk and, not bothering with the TV screen, pressed the appropriate button to allow her entry. Then he returned to the foyer, and with feet spread and arms crossed he waited for her appearance.

It wasn't long before the front door opened and she rushed inside, bringing with her a gust of leave-scented air. Vincent ignored the relief that rushed through him and let his bitterness take control. "Do you know what time it is?"

She paused momentarily before completing the task of securing the door. "No, not exactly." Turning, she slid up the sleeve of her coat and glanced at her watch, then bit her lip. "Sorry. I guess I lost track of the hours."

He didn't hear her answer because he was too busy focusing on her hair. "What in heaven's name have you done to yourself?"

She lifted a hand and combed her wind-tossed bangs over to the left. "I've had my hair cut."

"Butchered, you mean."

She lifted her chin, which, he noted, wasn't quite steady. "*I* like it."

"Why am I not surprised? These days you like anything you think I won't."

Her eyes grew very bright in the dimly lit room, and a part of him wanted to rush over to her, kiss away the hurt he knew he was causing her before tears spilled over her dusky lashes. But another, greater part of him was trapped in his rigidity.

Townsend cleared his throat. "Would you like me to bring you up a cup of tea, Miss Ceara? Dinner won't be ready for a few hours yet and it might soothe you after your long day."

"It wouldn't be too much trouble?"

Townsend assured her it wouldn't be, excused himself and retired to the kitchen. That left Vincent and Ceara in the uncomfortable silence. When she made a move to go toward the stairs, he stretched out his arm to block her way.

She froze, and though keeping her eyes trained on his arm, whispered, "How dare you? You have no right to speak to me that way. I'm sorry if I caused you concern—"

"Concern?" As successful as he was at keeping his voice low, it shook from anger, lingering fear for her and, yes, the ongoing longing that was tearing him apart. "That hardly begins to cover it. I've been going out of mind worrying about you."

"You needn't have troubled yourself so. As you can see, I'm perfectly fine."

"You're a guest in my house."

"I wasn't aware that meant I had to clear my every movement with you."

If she was intent on making a point, she couldn't have done it any more succinctly. Vincent clenched his teeth but managed to check his temper. "I'm not trying to be a jailer, Ceara, but all the protesting in the world won't make me stop caring." Helpless to resist, he lifted a hand to her hair, only to drop it and shake his head. "Why?"

"With the bandage off I was feeling self-conscious." She fingered the wisps at the back of her neck.

He hadn't meant to sound so critical before. Actually, he was surprised and disturbed at how much the style suited her. She looked more like a will-o'-the-wisp than ever, a wood nymph who was utterly desirable.

"Can we talk?" he asked gently.

"Isn't that what we're doing?"

He sighed. "Take off your coat and come talk to me."

After a slight hesitation, she slid out of the wool covering and placed it on the railing's round newel cap. Casting him a wary glance, she passed him and entered his study. Vincent, feeling emotionally flogged, followed. At least, he reassured himself, from this angle he could admire her without being resented. Her tailored blouse and black skirt enhanced the fluid lines of her body. Ceara had the legs for the short skirts, once again back in style, but he was grateful she preferred a more conservative length. He hated thinking of the men who no doubt leered at her regardless.

"What did the doctor say?" he asked, carefully closing the double doors behind them.

"Everything looks fine."

"I'm glad." He turned to face her. "And you had no trouble driving?"

She eyed the shut door before meeting his gaze. "I admit I'm tired, but then I have good cause to be."

"A provocative statement."

"I didn't mean to be, but...oh, Vincent, you'll never guess what happened to me today." Clasping her hands before her, she took a step toward him, and for the first time in ages he saw the excitement she used to exhibit when sharing something special with him. "I think I'm going to buy a business. Well, it's actually a house, but it's a house that's been converted into a business. You have to see it. I have such plans! All the way back here ideas were racing through my mind."

"But you have a business," Vincent replied, trying to make sense of what he was hearing. "The publishing firm may have gone public, but you hold a considerable share of the stock."

"Yes, of course. And I do plan to take a seat on the board, but assuming any greater role...it's not *me*. I want something that's more intimate, something that's all mine." She took a deep breath. "I'm buying a bookstore."

"Are you." It wasn't a question. He had no doubt he had heard correctly; he just didn't know what to make of it. A million and one questions came to mind, but he didn't know which to ask first. He leaned back against the door and crossed his arms. "Where?"

She told him. "Do you know it?"

"I may have passed it once, although as you know, Townsend runs most of my errands for me."

"But you must have seen it. It has the most glorious garden out front and the house itself is like something out of a fairy tale. The inside's in wonderful condition, although it does need some sprucing up. The bookcases and shelving are reliable. Boone did the carpentry himself.''

''Boone?''

''Mr. Tolliver. He and his sister established the business. Naomi died recently and so, since he doesn't feel he can manage on his own, Boone's selling out. When you first meet him, he can be somewhat gruff, but once he begins to trust you . . .''

''I think what's important is that *he's* trustworthy.''

''Vincent . . . I've given him a deposit.''

He couldn't believe what he was hearing. ''You've what? Have you lost your mind? You spend an hour or two seeing only what this man wants you to see, and based on that you make a legal commitment? Have you seen his financial records? Have you spoken to his creditors? What if there's a lien against the business or the house?''

''I'll have Dad's...my attorney can check on all that and make sure everything is handled properly.''

''But you haven't given yourself time to think this through. For one thing, you live in Manhattan. You can't tell me you're going to commute to Mapleton every day?''

''Of course not. I'm going to move there. The second floor remains as living quarters. I'll be perfectly happy.''

But Vincent wasn't happy at all. He knew he should take heart in the fact that she would be all the closer; however, it didn't matter to him whether she was in New York City or across the street. The point she was making perfectly clear was that she had no intention of staying here with him. It was a revelation that turned his world dark and desolate and his mood dour.

"I've been thinking," she continued, beginning to wander around the room, her face bright with hope and youthful enthusiasm. "I could expand on the concept Naomi had of providing refreshments and monthly readings for her customers. I was thinking of expanding it to a weekly thing, hopefully creating an atmosphere not unlike the old salons. It might even work to have seasonal cocktail parties and invite prominent authors who have books scheduled for release in that quarter. The one thing I do have, thanks to my father, is plenty of contacts. What do you think? Isn't it a fabulous idea?"

"More like a potential disaster, and a costly one at that. Mapleton isn't exactly Stamford, Ceara. What writer is going to traipse all the way up here to sign a half-dozen books for the local celebrity hounds?"

"These wouldn't be groupies. I'm talking about serious readers and book collectors."

"You might as well be searching for dinosaurs."

"It would work!"

"It's a pipe dream."

She stopped in the middle of the room and stared at him, the disappointment and hurt turning her eyes smoky and opaque. "You're being deliberately cruel."

"It's cruel to warn you of the pitfalls you're facing?"

"There would be pitfalls in anything I chose to do. What's your suggestion—that I sit in my apartment, eat petits fours and deposit my trust fund checks in my account?" Ceara shook her head. "And you're the man who said he would never ask anyone to be less than all they could be. I'm not a princess to be kept on a pedestal out of harm's way, Vincent. I have just as much right as anyone else to live my life, make my mistakes and have the satisfaction of reaching for dreams the way other people do.''

''Fine,'' he lashed out, unable to keep his temper from gaining control. ''Throw your money away. Heaven knows you can afford it.''

Swift color flooded her too-pale cheeks. ''Just like that,'' she said with a snap of her fingers, ''you're assuming I'm going to fail?''

''I didn't necessarily mean that.''

''You did. Now at least have the courtesy of not trying to sugarcoat it.'' She stalked around him and reached for the doorknob. ''And kindly get out of my way. I'd like to wash up before Townsend brings my tea.''

''Damn it, Ceara, don't close down on me like this.''

She stared at the shoulder seam of his black boatman's sweater. ''It's obvious we have nothing more to say to each other.''

''I have plenty.''

''Not anything I care to hear.''

''You will,'' he ground out, sliding an arm around her waist and bringing her against him. Without giving her an opportunity to catch her breath he claimed her mouth with his.

It hadn't been his intention to be rough or abrupt, but he couldn't stand this any longer. All her talk about businesses and changing residences...*plans,* when where she belonged was here with him. She was driving him mad, mad to the point that he let himself forget he had always wanted their first intimate kiss to be perfect, a bestowal from the heart, a joining of their souls. Hurt and fear wiped that away and left only need, a need to recapture what he knew he was losing.

He kissed her with all his pent-up frustration and hunger, feeling his teeth bite into the tender flesh of her lip, his fingers brand her with his heat as well as his strength. Even when she beat against his shoulders and whimpered to stop his fierce assault on her mouth, he knew only the blinding need to have and to hold.

"No," she moaned, finally succeeding in wrenching her head back.

Given access to the sensitive length of her throat, Vincent plundered the silky, fragrant spot with the appetite of a man denied nourishment too long. Need blinded him, loneliness made him deaf to her protests, but it was his all-consuming love that induced him to spin them both around and trap her between himself and the door.

Never had they been closer; never had he wanted her more. It was in that moment, however, when he raised his head to tell her so, that he saw the absolute terror on her face. Seeing himself through her eyes, he suddenly experienced the full impact of what he had done, was doing.

Ever so slowly he released his hold. She slid back to where her feet once again touched the carpet. Aware her entire body was trembling and chilled, he thought the cold couldn't possibly be as fatal as the dread seeping into his heart.

Self-revulsion filled him. All those years of regret, he thought, all his self-imposed solitary confinement and he hadn't learned a thing from it. In a moment of lost control he had almost violated the one person he cherished most on earth. He *was* a monster.

"L-let me go."

He held Ceara's gaze. Time stopped. Hearts pounded. Lungs fought for breath. Seeing there were no

words to repair what he had done, he dropped his arm
to his sides.

Instantly Ceara grappled behind her for the door
knob. "In the morning I—I'll make arrangements to
have my things moved to the inn. Thank you for making it such an e-easy decision, after all."

All Vincent could do was shut his eyes and let her go.
It was the only form of apology he knew she would accept from him.

Chapter Seven

On the second Friday in October Ceara signed the papers and became the legal owner of the house and business at 117 West Park Lane. She promptly took down the sign that read The Book Place and had Boone affix the brass nameplate marked House of Books she had specially made for over the front entranceway. Afterward she insisted on serving Boone and her attorney, Dennis Armistead, a lunch prepared courtesy of the ladies at the Lemon Tree and toasting the event with champagne.

It was late afternoon when she walked Dennis to his car. The sun was already behind the house and casting long shadows. A persistent, crisp breeze was bringing a close to what had been a glorious Indian summer day. Ceara hugged her cashmere shawl closer and smiled as Dennis teased her about the hardly significant usefulness of the front gate latch.

At thirty-four he was an attractive man, all charm and sunny good looks. A full partner in the firm established by his father, he was as aware as she was that once their parents had hoped of a romance blossoming between them. Instead they were comfortable but unromantic friends.

"Thanks for doing this for me," she told him, picking up on their previous discussion about his taking over the responsibility of being her personal legal counsel, as his father had been her father's.

"Well, as I warned you, real estate isn't my bailiwick, but an associate helped me over the things I had questions on, so I actually ended up enjoying the change. It's to your credit that you and Tolliver were able to simplify the deal." He placed his briefcase in the car and shut the passenger door before considering Ceara with eyes as brown as her own. "I can't deny the place seems to have potential, but I have to repeat that I'm somewhat concerned about your plans to stay here by yourself."

"I told you, I'm not really alone," Ceara insisted. "Boone's been living in the apartment over the garage."

"In case you need someone to point it out to you, the man's not exactly a teddy bear."

"Don't let his gruffness fool you. He's a dear. In the past two weeks I've learned a great deal about and from him. I think we're going to get along wonderfully."

"You and your affection for eccentric types."

Ceara knew exactly who else he was referring to and quickly changed the subject. "You will come for the grand opening if I send you an invitation?"

Dennis's frown transformed into a wry smile and he nodded. "What would it look like if I turned down my favorite client's party? Now that's something I know will be a success. You've always put on the most interesting parties of anyone I know.''

''I'll share my secret. Keep the invitation list diverse, the liquid refreshment plentiful and the food nothing that requires forks or spoons. You may pass that on to Meryl with my blessings.''

He groaned playfully. ''You're so subtle.''

''Will you bring her? It's been ages since we've had a chance to visit.''

''It's a deal. If you'll promise to phone me should anything problematic arise—even if it's only a need for a shoulder to cry on.''

Ceara patted his arm and rose on tiptoe to kiss his cheek. ''I hired you for your mind, not your capacity to worry about me.''

Despite an irreverent grunt, his look was speculative. ''You know, you're changing. It's more than the hair—which, may I say again, is great. You're gaining a new maturity. Not that you weren't mature before. You couldn't help it moving in the same circles Carson did. But there was always something unaffected about you. It was as if you lived in your own dreamworld. But—'' he smiled ''—I believe Sleeping Beauty is awake now.''

''All it took was a nosedive into reality,'' she muttered.

''Hmm...that sounds interesting. Want to talk about it?''

''Not unless you care to explain why you and Meryl haven't set a date for the wedding yet.''

She watched Dennis's handsome face turn an interesting and telling shade of pink. ''You are getting tougher. All right, I'll keep my nose to myself. Just one question—have you heard from the Prince of Spooks lately?''

Ceara couldn't help it; her smile wilted with the sharp spasm of pain that sliced through her. ''Dennis...be nice.''

''Ask for the moon, why don't you? I've sat across from him at one negotiation table too many. He's unmerciful...and eerie. And that attorney of his—the guy looks more like a gnome living in one of New York City's underground systems.''

''You're just annoyed that you and your father haven't yet succeeded in outmaneuvering them.'' Ceara considered Dennis's two-tone gray tie and realized she had never seen Vincent in one. He preferred more comfortable, sensual clothing like sweaters, especially turtlenecks. ''At any rate, I haven't seen him, and I really don't expect to. We've...grown apart. It's sad but true, nonetheless.''

Her friend's eyes narrowed with interest. ''No wonder you seem so different. Professional attitudes aside, I am aware of how close you two have been. For your sake, I'm sorry. Just don't forget that relationships have to experience growing pains if they're to go anywhere.''

He bent to kiss her cheek, then rounded the car and climbed in. When he eased his sedan out of its parking slot, Ceara waved one last time and turned back toward the house. Boone's Halloween decorations caught her eye and momentarily eased her troubled heart. Her favorite was the ghost chasing the straw man. They were surrounded by numerous pumpkins. Soon she would help Boone carve the largest of the gourds for the Halloween ghost story party they would be hosting for the local children, even though the store wouldn't officially open until December.

It was as she was climbing the stairs that Ceara experienced a unique but familiar feeling. She was being watched. That in itself wasn't unusual; as the new person in town, it was an inevitable situation, one only time would solve. No, she thought, this was different; and when she heard a vehicle behind her, she glanced over her shoulder in time to see a black Jeep-type vehicle drive by, turn north at the corner and disappear around the park's dense cluster of hemlocks.

Her heart leaped against her breast. Vincent? There was no reason to believe it should have been him, especially at this time of day when he was probably at home hard at work. He had deadlines, they weren't talking, and yet the car had been like his, and as far as she could tell from this distance, there had been only one person inside.

"Vincent..." A flood of emotions swept over her: she missed him; she was exasperated with him...if that was him, why hadn't he stopped? A foolish question, she told herself with her next breath.

Townsend had come by last week to return a book of poetry she had forgotten to pack, and a few days later just because he had been in town running errands. Excuses. She could identify them for what they were and adored him for it. But from her former closest friend and soul mate there had been nothing. No wonder her imagination was working overtime.

Once again hugging her shawl close, Ceara hurried inside, feeling somewhat embarrassed and not a little sorry for herself. At least, she thought, shutting and bolting the door behind her, she didn't have to explain those feelings to anyone. But how nice it would be to

have someone to talk them over with ... someone like
Vincent.

"Goodbye! Thank you for coming and happy Halloween!"

Balancing the tray bearing a remaining caramel apple in one hand, Ceara waved at her departing guests
with her other. Next year, she decided as she watched a
skeleton and an adorable white bunny finally locate
their parent in the group of adults and costumed children swarming the outer sidewalk, she would come up
with a better costume for herself. The gypsy outfit she
was wearing wasn't bad, but how much creativity did it
take to slip on an off-the-shoulder fuchsia leotard, stitch
layers of colorful crepe paper to an old black gathered
skirt and slip on almost every piece of gold and silver
jewelry she owned? Still, she'd had fun, and the house,
in its present state of half-painted rooms, draped paint
cloth and general disarray—along with the flickering
candles inside jack-o'-lanterns—had been perfect for
the haunted house effect she had wanted for her eager
audience.

With a last wave she returned inside, shivering as she
quickly closed out the damp mist and cold. There was
another good reason to have had the party. The children may have eaten just as much junk food as they
would have during trick-or-treating, but their chances
of catching a cold were now less likely than if they had
been running from door to door. And, she thought with
a silent chuckle as she placed her tray on the cashier's
desk, the caramel apples they all received as a parting
gift would linger on their tastebuds long after they
brushed their teeth and were tucked cozily into their
beds.

"Want me to go blow out the candles outside?" Boone asked from the hallway.

Dressed as some nameless ghoul, his face would have looked tired even without the flour dusting she had added with a powder puff. Ceara knew he'd had as good a time with the children as she had—despite all his previous grumbling about the resulting mess they had to look forward to—just as she could see that he was worn-out.

"I'll take care of it as soon as I straighten up a few things here. Why don't you go on to bed?"

"Trying to get rid of me?"

"Trying to let you get some rest after what's been a full day for both of us. Don't worry. I'm not going to clean up much. I just like to have a few minutes alone after a party to unwind."

If not totally convinced, he did look tempted. "Guess Moss is hiding upstairs having a coronary after being tugged in all directions by them young'uns."

"Actually, I think he loved the attention. He's in his favorite observation post." Ceara indicated the top of the bookcase behind the cashier's counter.

As if he understood exactly what was going on, the Persian peered over the high trim and offered a whimsical greeting. At first Ceara hadn't been thrilled with the prospect of living with a cat determined to hover over her head when she dealt with customers, but in the past few days she had abandoned her attempts to keep him off there, even going so far as to give him one of her older shawls to make him more comfortable.

Boone muttered something under his breath about worthless animals having a better life than humans did, then shrugged. "Guess I'll go then. May be late in the morning. Ain't as young as I used to be, you know.

Back's been killing me with this damp weather. Need my rest. Unless you'll be wanting something done earlier?'' he added, his wild eyebrows hooking like question marks. ''I can be here anytime you say. Just give me the word.''

''There's nothing special going on tomorrow except more painting, which can wait. See you whenever,'' Ceara replied, knowing the man wanted sympathy and praise in the worst way. To hide her smile she stooped to pick up a cupcake wrapper from the floor, then tossed it into the trash container by the doorway to the hall. ''And, Boone,'' she added as he began to shuffle away, ''I really appreciate your help. The party wouldn't have been half the success it was without you. The children thought you were terrific.''

He looked momentarily flustered. Then he squared his shoulders, lifted his head and walked away, the bathroom tissue paper she had wrapped around him as part of his costume trailing behind like waving fingers. A strange but sweet man, Ceara thought with a wistful sigh.

She spent the next few minutes collecting cookie and cupcake crumbs and wiping up spilled punch, something she simply couldn't let go until morning. Confident that all her guests were gone, she stepped outside and went from pumpkin to pumpkin, blowing out the candles. The mist was a chilly caress on her bare shoulders and emphasized her solitude. She had come to feel safe in this friendly community, but tonight she was experiencing a poignant isolation she hadn't felt since the earliest days after leaving Vincent.

What was he doing tonight? Did he even pay attention to such things as Halloween? Except for knowing he was working on a new Bourne Rampal book, she hadn't a clue as to how it was going. There had been a time when he used to tell her, share particular frustrations over a turn in the storyline that wasn't working or ask her advice about a female character's motivation. For a while, after reading her father's journals, she had allowed herself to suspect it was all patronization. Now she simply grieved that she wouldn't have the benefit of all his insight to help her when she read his next release.

There was no sense in trying to convince herself that she would never again touch one of his books. He was a gifted writer. He cared about technique and language as much as he did the story. His self-deprecating remarks regarding his abilities were merely that. She knew he wrote, rewrote and edited himself mercilessly, and even when his books arrived on bookstore shelves, he put himself through various forms of hell because he could see flaws or at the least places where he would have done something differently. No, to deny herself his friendship and presence was one thing; to deny herself his work would be quite another.

The floodlights going off next door at the Lemon Tree snapped Ceara out of her daydreaming. Wrapping her arms around herself, she quickly climbed the steps, her bracelets and necklaces creating a uniquely lighthearted tune in the heavy silence.

Once in the front room, she went to the huge pumpkin in the bay window and blew out its candle. What a handful this one had been to carve and carry, and how the children had fussed over him. At the cashier's counter she leaned over a family of three. It was as she was taking a breath to blow out their candles that someone knocked at the door. Her lungs full, she spun around.

A silhouette of a tall dark figure was outlined in the half-glass door. Under any other circumstance the beveled and frosted panes would have made it impossible to determine much about who stood on the other side, except in this case. His coat or cape made his shoulders appear almost as wide as the door. Ceara knew that shape and dimension even in her dreams, and in a moment's flash of recognition relief merged with a different kind of trepidation.

Swallowing and resisting the impulse to press a hand to her thudding heart, she crossed the room, her gaze held mesmerized by eyes she couldn't yet delineate but felt boring into her. The sound of the dead bolt yielding was more like a blow of a battering ram, the turn of the doorknob was like a rusty dungeon hinge, and her heart, loudest of all, echoed in her ears like kettle drums.

He stood, the ultimate All Hallow's Eve visitor, dressed in black, his coat draped casually, artfully, over his shoulders that, as she had already noted, only added to his size. His black hair glistened with a fine dusting of raindrops, as did his face, telling Ceara that he must have been standing outside for a considerable time.

"I didn't mean to frighten you."

"You're out late."

"Restless souls are wandering tonight. It's not an evening for working."

It was a typical Dante response—half quip, half serious, and as a result, unsettling to Ceara's contradictory feelings about the man, her helpless attraction to him and her rational side's need to resist that attraction. She soon found out, however, that in any tug-of-war she still ended up in over her head.

"This is also a night when you don't show up on anyone's doorstep without letting them know whether you're here for a trick or treat," she replied, gripping the doorknob as if it were her anchor to reality.

"Except that I didn't come to threaten or beg but to offer."

"Excuse me?"

Before he could reply there was a soft mew from inside his coat followed by a low grumble behind her. Ceara didn't know where to look first. "I think you'd better come in before we have a street brawl on our hands." She stepped aside to let him enter and shut the door behind him. Placing herself between him and Moss, she demanded, "What's going on?"

"We've had a caller at the house." Vincent stretched out a hand, producing a ball of fur topped by two pointy ears, citron-green eyes and whiskers longer than the tail tucked between its hind legs. "Townsend found him in the garage. Can you take him?"

"That wasn't a parakeet you just heard behind me. Why can't you keep him? Overbooked?"

Vincent's lips curled slightly. "He's immune to closed doors, prefers human companionship to the bed Townsend made for him in the pantry, and is thoroughly inconsiderate of my work habits."

Ceara worked at interpreting that while fingering a dangling earring. She decided it came up promising but short. "That sounded more like an apology than a sales pitch."

"You've always had a gift for handling loners and outcasts," he said, his voice deepening to what could only be described as black velvet. "I thought he might be happier with you."

"But as you've already discovered I have a—" Moss sprang from his hiding place, leaped across the cashier's counter and onto the armrest of a chair near Vincent's elbow. With claws exposed he snagged Vincent's sweater and drew hand and kitten closer. The kitten scrambled from Vincent's palm and joined Moss in the chair. "Cat," Ceara concluded as the giant feline began to bathe the newcomer, who proceeded to curl back into a ball and purr contentedly.

She couldn't believe her eyes. Moss liked people well enough, but she had discovered that if he even saw another cat through the safety of the front window, he began howling like a demon. "This is impossible. Moss is extremely territorial. You called yours a he, right? Why isn't there fur flying and ungodly sounds filling the house?"

"I told you, this is a night for the unusual."

She should have known better than to ask him. Moistening her lips, she warned, "I can't make any promises."

"Have I asked for any?"

"If it doesn't work out, you'll have to take him back. I won't be the one to take him to a shelter. I would, however, check around to see if someone could offer him a home."

"It's more than a man has a right to ask."

Ceara glanced down at the two animals because it was much safer than looking at Vincent while trying to analyze what else she was hearing in his voice besides gratitude. Never mind, she told herself. It was best not to risk guessing. First thing in the morning she would have a chat with Boone to make sure Moss was a male as she had assumed. Vincent was obviously not going to be any help there, and it wouldn't be wise to forget how some people said "he" or "it" no matter what the sex of an animal.

"All right, he can stay, only how I let you talk me into this I'll never know," she muttered, not caring if she sounded ungracious or otherwise.

"Speaking on behalf of both Townsend and myself, thank you."

She let that one pass and waited for him to make a move to leave. He didn't, and that prompted a new assault on her nerves. But regardless of what his presence did to her rational side, she couldn't deny that as far as her heart was concerned, it was a relief to see him again.

"How are you?" she asked, because nothing else seemed appropriate or enough.

"I've spent so many years hiding my thoughts and feelings," he began quietly, "I'm not sure how to begin telling you."

She searched for the pockets in her skirt, remembering belatedly that she didn't have any. There was no place to hide her heart, either. "Well . . . I suppose as a beginning form of honesty that's very nice."

"Why don't you tell me. How do I look?"

That wasn't easy either because she didn't want to acknowledge she saw stark changes or analyze what they meant. There were dark shadows under his eyes, a tautness at his cheekbones, tension and weariness in his entire bearing. A droplet of water trickled down his cheek and made her itch to stroke it away.

"You look wet . . . tired . . . and chilled to the bone. How long have you been standing outside?" she finally asked.

"I wasn't paying attention to the time, only the need to see you."

"You didn't have to wait until everyone went home," she said, suddenly needing to fill the room with chatter. "The children would have loved playing with the kitten, since there was only so much of Moss to go around." When he cocked an eyebrow at her, she exhaled in gentle exasperation. "They were just children, Vincent. Your aversion to dealing with the world in general is one thing, but...children?"

"Children sometimes see more than adults do. I was feeling selfish. I wanted to see you alone."

Ceara's legs went boneless and her temperature soared. Wanting desperately to cross the space separating them and be held in his strong arms, she smoothed her skirt to dry her damp palms. But she couldn't reply. The right words wouldn't come.

He dropped his gaze to her bare shoulders, her breasts, before considering her skirt. "Interesting costume. A one-hundred-eighty-degree reversal from your own personality."

"Somehow I didn't see a vestal virgin going over well with my guests," she drawled, grateful for the change of focus, regardless of how personal it remained. "Considering their age group, I figured it would be a waste of symbolism."

"So what did you do, enchant them by reading their palms and brewing them magic potions to use on their parents and teachers?"

She allowed herself a smile. "I told ghost stories. There were a few older children who remained doubtful until I had Boone come in—costumed, of course—at a strategic moment. I think they all went home properly spooked."

"Things are working out between the two of you?" he ventured.

"I think they are. Of course, the place still needs a lot of work if I'm going to achieve the look I want, and we've only started."

He glanced around. "Good. Things look...interesting."

As compliments went, it was more than she had been expecting from him, and yet she was disappointed. She loved the house, and in the bottom of her heart she had been hoping his presence meant he'd had a change of heart and might now want to support her in her venture. Clearly she would be making a mistake to assume so much.

Lifting her chin, she told him, "I'd show you around, however, it is late."

"Of course. Perhaps on another occasion."

"The next time you're passing through town."

"Earlier, naturally. After all, one can see so much better in daylight."

"That would help."

"And at the same time wouldn't leave you feeling so vulnerable."

She had stepped innocently and unthinkingly into his trap. Ceara could see it in the grim look on his face and the stiffness of his bearing. "That wasn't fair," she replied, trying to maintain her equanimity. "But, all right, I'll admit it. Being alone with you isn't as easy as it used to be."

"Because of what happened the night...the last time we were together?"

"We both know it began long before that, but for the sake of argument, that will do."

"And what if I promised you it would never happen again?"

She glanced away because the vehemence in his voice and eyes was too penetrating, too coercive to resist. "You can't, because it will happen. It always will as long as you continue feeling guilty for wanting what you think you don't deserve or have a right to reach for. I understand that. What I can't bear is having you make me feel as though *I* would be making a mistake to listen to you."

He drew a deep breath and closed his eyes. "I just . . . miss you, Ceara."

It was the same for her. That was the hell of it. But, dear God, she wouldn't cry; nor would she let him undo what she had managed to achieve for herself.

He seemed disappointed in her silence and at a loss for anything to say. Just when Ceara was sure he was ready to give up and retreat, he happened to glance somewhere over her shoulder. In the next instant he stepped around her and went to the cashier counter where he picked up the caramel apple.

"I saw the children with these. They were singing your praises while their parents muttered about dentist bills."

It was the strangest thing to hear him say, but despite everything Ceara couldn't resist a smile. "No doubt. My father wasn't any different, but that didn't stop me from getting hold of one whenever I could. That's what prompted me to make them. A child should be allowed a few risks in order to store up memories. Our youth passes so quickly. Before you know it there's no more room for impetuosity and simple fun, and that's so sad."

"Mmm." Vincent turned the stick in his fingers, and the caramel glowed with wicked temptation in the flickering lights. "Is this one yours?"

"No. Boone and I overdosed on caramel while lick-ing the pot. That one's just an extra. A rather close call, I'm afraid. Next year I'll have to remember to estimate more liberally."

"May I have it?"

"What?" Ceara stared, not sure she had heard him correctly.

"Yes. I meant it."

"But... well, go ahead if you want."

He lifted it to his nose and drew in another deep breath. "Hot summer wind...sawdust, sweat...and deafening noise." He returned to stand beside her. "That's what these remind me of."

Although she was intrigued, Ceara wrinkled her nose. "I'm not sure that sounds very pleasant."

"Pleasant doesn't begin to describe it. I'm talking about the first and only time I've ever been to the cir-cus. It was the most innocent and happy day of my life. My mother took me. She did it on the sly when my fa-ther was in Boston for a seminar or something. I was only eight, so the particulars escape me. All I remem-ber was sensing he wouldn't have approved. It was the money, I think. Things were tight then, and as much as I loved and respected my father, he didn't have what you would call a well-rounded sense of humor."

"No doubt that's where you inherited yours," Ceara drawled.

Vincent smiled, clearly taking no offense. "Strange. I'd forgotten the story until now."

He bit into the apple, his white teeth sinking past caramel and breaking into the fruit's juicy center. The crunching sound, the way he closed his eyes, the low, sexy moan that rose from deep in his chest...it all made Ceara's mouth water.

"Thank you for this," he murmured, and quickly leaned close to share the sweet-tart flavor of caramel and apple through a deliberate but tender kiss. "And thank you for bringing back a happy memory of my childhood," he whispered gruffly.

Then, before Ceara could think of an appropriate if not intelligent reply, he let himself out. She followed like a sleepwalker and stood on the landing, watching until he crossed the street and blended in with the shadowy images of the hemlocks and juniper in the park. How strange, she mused, so much so that she wouldn't be surprised to realize she had just dreamed this whole thing.

With a shake of her head she glanced over her shoulder. No, it hadn't been a fantasy. Not only was the tray empty, the newest member of the household had leaped up on the counter and was licking caramel off the foil.

Quickly locking up, she hurried over to the kitten and scooped him up. "I don't suppose you'd like to interpret any of that for me?" she murmured, nuzzling him. But the kitten merely curled more comfortably against her and purred louder. "Oh, Vincent," she sighed, stroking her cheek against its fur, "just when I think I might begin to start getting over you. The least you could have done is told me this little one's name."

Chapter Eight

She named the cat Puck after her favorite mischievous character in Shakespeare's *A Midsummer Night's Dream,* and after only a day of shadowing the two, she accepted it wasn't a fluke—Moss had indeed taken to the kitten. The older feline set about to teach him every hiding spot in the house, leaving Ceara to return to her projects.

October drifted into November, and one by one the rooms were completed. She had plenty of interruptions as neighbors, former patrons, potential new ones and the merely curious stopped by to visit. With each new acquaintance her enthusiasm grew. People began signing up for her monthly readings, and a few submitted applications for the salesclerk position. Ceara gave those individuals as much time as she could because, even though she wanted to hire all of them, she had a set idea of what she wanted out of an employee. In addition, she was also aware it took a canny reader as much as a true lover of the printed word to be a helpful bookseller.

In the evenings after dinner she returned to complete whatever goal she had set that day. Later, after a long, bubbly soak in the tub, she would sit at the Victorian desk she'd had freighted over from the Manhattan apartment before subleasing it, and go through her mail. She also dropped notes to friends at the publishing house, thanking them for their get-well cards and explaining her reasons for leaving her position there. Naturally she always added an invitation to visit.

She was working on one of those notes one evening, a few days after Halloween, when a sound from downstairs caught her attention. The eerie howl had the hairs at the back of her neck rising, and she fingered the collar of her yellow angora robe. It was Moss; she could tell that much. But why was he so upset?

Only she was around to investigate.

She congratulated herself for always leaving on a Tiffany-style lamp in the bay window. It provided enough light to get downstairs. Midway, she saw Moss standing on the bottom step, his back arched, his hair standing on end and Puck nowhere to be seen. When she saw the figure outlined against the front door's glass, she didn't blame the kitten.

A burglar!

But burglars didn't knock politely. Nor did they carry what she soon discerned upon closer inspection was a gift basket.

Ceara hurried to unbolt the door. "Do you know what time it is?" she demanded of Vincent in a loud whisper.

"I saw the light on upstairs."

He had to have circled her house to do that. "You're lucky Boone didn't see you and come after you with a broom, or worse, call the police." Exasperated and unable to deny she was relieved to see him, Ceara motioned him inside.

He looked wonderful but tired, something his characteristic black attire only accentuated. She couldn't help worry what he was doing to himself, but forced herself to focus on why he had come. "What's that?" she asked, nodding at the basket.

"I couldn't ask you to take in another mouth to feed without assisting in its support, could I?"

She inspected the contents of the basket, which included numerous varieties of gourmet cat food, and shot him a mild look. "Vincent, Puck weighs all of twenty-six ounces. He and Moss could live off this for weeks *and* open a soup kitchen on the side. And where did you find such things?" she added, aware nothing of the kind was available in their rural town, quaint though it was.

"I sent Townsend to Stamford . . . er, you've named it?"

"What did you think I would do—issue him a number?" she drawled before shaking her head over the assortment. "Thank you, but you could have asked Townsend to bring this next time he was in town."

"I needed to see you myself."

Needed. There was that seductive word again, urging her to reach for what she had to remember would be a mistake. It hurt that he did everything to avoid meeting Boone or Nydia and Mr. Pritchard, the former homemaker and retired schoolteacher she had hired to work part-time at the store. Maybe she did continue to miss him, to feel only fully complete when she was with him. But she was determined to prove she could succeed here. It was important that he recognize as much.

"Vincent, this isn't fair," she sighed, too aware also of her fresh-scrubbed face, the thick socks on her feet and the floral print teddy she wore beneath her robe. How long could either of them ignore the deepening undercurrents stirring between them? Where once spiritual and intellectual friendship was the binding cord of their connection, now there was no denying the growing intensity of their sexual awareness of each other. "You're not being fair."

"It's been a long time since I've had any reason to bother," he admitted. "But I'm trying to relearn the concept. Will you be patient with me as I do?"

Was he reaching for the impossible? Were they doomed to be star-crossed lovers, forever desiring something that couldn't be? She could never become the recluse Vincent was any more than she could watch him punish himself for his past mistakes, while he was clearly having difficulties in accepting her changes.

Ceara reached up and touched his cheek. In response Vincent captured her hand and brought it to his mouth, pressing an ardent kiss into her palm.

"You've never looked more enchanting," he whispered, and abruptly spun away and let himself out.

Speechless, torn by a bittersweet yearning, Ceara pressed her forehead against the shut door. She stayed that way until she could no longer hear the sound of his car as he drove away.

As if he was testing her resolve, Ceara didn't see him for a full week after that. In a way she was relieved. Things were so hectic that she needed the time to concentrate. But because of the surprise she had found at the bottom of the basket, she couldn't help but wonder and worry. In time for her birthday he had tucked in a red velvet box. Inside was a gold unicorn pendant on an equally exquisite chain.

She was thinking about the gift and her awkward thank-you note one evening as she carried a sack of trash out. After piling it on top of the others, she wandered into the backyard and gazed up at the sky. With the lights already off in Boone's quarters and at the Lemon Tree, she could see part of the Milky Way. It filled her with wonder and reminded her of her insignificance . . . until she saw the meteor streak across the sky.

She smiled, remembering how her father once explained them as angels carrying miracles to earth. This meteor was heading in the direction of Vincent's house. If ever there was someone in need of an angel's care, she thought, touching her pendant as she headed back inside, it was . . . She almost screamed when she saw the figure standing in the driveway.

"Did you make a wish?"

"Vincent . . ." she said, wondering if the man was part warlock. As usual, he was dressed in black, and the starkness made the blooming potted plant he held all the more noticeable and stunning. She approached him on legs that felt unfamiliar and shaky. "I was just thinking about you."

"What a coincidence. I think about you all the time."

Drawn by some invisible hand, she crossed to him, focusing on the plant. Camellias. As white and pure as the stars. "They're lovely," she breathed, stroking a perfect petal. "But you mustn't keep bringing gifts."

"This is no gift. It's a necessity. After studying your front window, I came to the conclusion it lacked something."

How could she argue when he was right? For days now she had been pondering what was wrong with the books and lamp arranged painstakingly in her window. Thanking him, she gave up trying not to shiver from the cold that, unthwarted by her teal velour jumpsuit, sliced through her. "Let's go inside before we freeze. I was about to indulge in a nightcap of cappuccino. You can join me."

"I could smell it as I came past the door," Vincent admitted wryly, "and was hoping you'd ask."

But something happened once they were in her kitchen and the door was closed. The big, spacious room suddenly seemed half its normal size and too dark with only the hurricane lamp lit on the dinette table. The comfortable silence was deafening and awkward. Awareness vibrated from the very walls.

Ceara invited him to sit down at the table, where she placed the plant. She tried not to focus on how romantic the setting was and concentrate on serving. "How've you been? Working hard, no doubt. I hope not too hard," she said cheerfully—too cheerfully, she thought with an inner wince.

His replies were polite but reserved; she could tell he was no longer comfortable, either. Sitting down made things worse. The table seemed abysmally small for someone his size, and their elbows and knees were no more than a breath apart.

Vincent eagerly lifted his demitasse and tasted the rich concoction. Ceara wanted to do the same but found herself helpless as she watched his lips touch the cup's rim and draw creamy froth into his mouth. She felt his pleasure wash over her.

His hands suddenly trembled and he put down the cup and stared at it. "Don't do that," he pleaded. "Not unless you're ready for the consequences."

She shook her head, too dazed to understand. "Do what?"

"Stare at me. Do you have any idea how expressive your face is?" Without waiting for her to respond he continued. "You were watching me as though you wished you were the one I was ... holding ... tasting."

It was true, but that didn't stop her from being embarrassed. It took her a moment to find her voice. "I'm sorry. I know that must make you think I'm contradicting everything I've been asserting."

"No. I understand what you're trying to do for yourself. But you need to understand that though I intend to find my place in that world ... I'm only human."

What could she say in reply to that? She wasn't exactly surprised; a man didn't keep calling if he didn't have something on his mind. It would help, however, if she knew what it was ... and if, just once, he didn't play night owl. "I won't revert back to old patterns, Vincent," she warned, "and I'll never allow myself to be anyone's possession again."

"Not my possession," he agreed, plucking a camellia from the bush and carrying it to her lips. "But you are my obsession. Nothing can change that, Ceara, especially now when I'm realizing how strong you had to be to stand up to me ... and win."

"I don't feel much like a winner," she replied breathlessly.

"You should. You're proving you were right and I was wrong."

"You're talking in riddles tonight."

Ever so slowly he stroked the white petals across her bottom lip, then over her chin and down her throat. Unable to breathe, Ceara trembled as he trailed a path past the base of her throat to the farthermost V of her jumpsuit where the pendant rested.

"Right again." Abruptly he rose. "And I'll confess something else. I've changed my mind. I'd rather go to bed with the taste of you on my lips," he murmured, bending to brush his mouth against hers. "A belated happy birthday, my Ceara."

Far into the night as she lay wide-awake in her bed Ceara could feel his kiss and see the camellia he'd taken with him, held protectively in his big hand.

The scene stayed with her for days. If it wasn't for the pressure of trying to finish readying her store for the grand opening, she was sure she would have lost her mind. Finally the time for restacking the mainstream fiction room had come. As with all the rest, the books had been boxed away in alphabetical order, the way they had been previously shelved. Naomi's policing of the system, however, hadn't been absolute, and in addition to haphazard filing, there were often multiple copies of books Ceara knew would never sell.

It was as she was sitting on the floor between aisles stacking those extras into boxes she planned to donate to senior citizen centers that she heard someone behind her. Certain it was Boone coming to ask, or else grumble, about something, she reached out her hand. "Can you pass me the short stack on the floor? They go into this donation box, too."

Instead of the books she felt something long, slender and not paper. With a gasp she swiveled around. No, it wasn't Boone standing there but Vincent, and instead of handing her books, he had presented her with a long-stemmed white rose.

"Hello," he murmured conversationally, as though they hadn't shared a strange conversation days ago, and that it was perfectly normal for him to be here this hour of day. He removed his sunglasses and scooped up the volumes she had indicated. "Hmm. None of mine, I see. But all means, donate them."

Ceara automatically accepted the novels, but her heart was slow in recovering from her shock. "You scared me half to—oh, this is lovely." Aware she was making no sense whatsoever, she took a moment to enjoy the fragile scent of the blossom. "I'm afraid to ask what trouble you went to in order to find a white one at this time of year."

"Who knows? It might prove a wise investment to own one's own floral business." At her shocked look he grinned. "Only teasing. Are you coming up here, or am I going down there?"

Vincent Dante making jokes and sitting on the floor, even if it was carpeted in new smoky-blue luxurious pile and he was in jeans, had her scrambling to her feet. "What are you doing here?" she demanded, using her free hand to tug down her long peacock-blue sweater over her black leggings. *Wouldn't you know it?* she fumed, feeling self-conscious. *The one day I pay absolutely no attention to my appearance and he decides to stray from routine, too.* He was dressed somewhat out of character himself. She had never seen that black leather bomber jacket, and its blatant masculine effect only added to her flustered state.

"I thought that was pretty obvious," he said, pocketing the sunglasses.

"May I point out it's barely eleven in the morning?"

His smile was as amused as it was seductive. "Concerned that I may go up in smoke? You've seen me in daylight enough times to know I'm no vampire."

And she was about the only one who *was* convinced, she mused dryly. "But not too many days ago you admitted your current novel wasn't going well."

"Mmm . . ."

"Have things changed?"

"Not a whit."

"Oh, Vincent . . . I'm so looking forward to reading about Bourne Rampal again. Cartographer turned treasure-hunting adventurer—he's such a colorful character, and you've neglected giving him another story for too long. What's wrong now?"

"He's getting old," Vincent muttered, his voice taking on an edge of sarcasm. "At least too old for having a fling with whichever damsel in distress this latest adventure drops into his path."

"For heaven's sake, he's only your age."

"Thank you for reminding me."

Although it triggered some inner satisfaction to hear he couldn't see someone like himself having casual affairs, either, Ceara wasn't certain how to comment. "Maybe you just haven't found him the right heroine yet."

"I've come to the same conclusion." He eyed her from beneath stark eyebrows. "He wants Anna."

Her pulse accelerated to a sprinter's beat. "You married Anna off to Matthew, and two adventures later you mentioned they moved to England where Matthew took a post with another museum." She knew it was irrational to have grown so close to a pair of fictional characters, but she had somehow seen parallels between Anna's unrequited love for Bourne and her own feelings for Vincent.

"Obviously Bourne's not as content on his New England island as he used to be."

"If his feelings are as strong as you seem to be suggesting, he would have kept track of her in his own way."

"What if he has?"

Pinpricks of excitement raced up Ceara's arms; her imagination was stirred. What, indeed? "All right... maybe that's why he knows her husband's been killed. The killers could turn out to be the same men who've robbed his friend of the ancient Spanish map you say you have him searching for in your current book."

This time Vincent was the one who grew reflective. Frowning, he stroked his chin. "Don't you think that would seem somewhat contrived? Besides, with good old sensible Matthew being a curator of a rather specialized museum, it's not likely he'd become involved."

True, Ceara thought, still heartbroken that he had made Bourne send Anna back to kind but dull Matthew. "Fine," she replied, determined to correct the matter. "But what if his hobby remains ancient maps, just as it was Anna's father's, and what if he can't resist when an acquaintance asks him to authenticate a map for another friend? He realizes what he has, gets too nosy about the map's provenance and meets with an unfortunate accident."

"Hmm... that's interesting. But it would be problematic if he had the map on him when he's killed,"

Vincent added thoughtfully. "After all, then the search would be over."

"Matthew was uninspiring in matters of the heart, but professionally he was clever. He would have tucked it away someplace secure. So this acquaintance steps in to offer Anna his heartfelt sympathies, not to mention his assistance, hoping for an opportunity to hunt for it.'

"And following the thieves' trail to England, Bourne connects this friend to the thieves and happens to arrive in time to see the acquaintance with Anna." He leaned back his head and uttered a sigh of relief. "I might work."

Ceara, however, had a new concern. "You're not going to make him suspect her of collaborating again, are you? That would be redundant."

"Not to mention hardly indicative of his feelings for her, eh? No, he'll have his hands full trying to keep her pretty nose out of trouble . . . especially since she won't buy the idea that this high-profile acquaintance could be dabbling in black-market antiquities."

"Only because she's not a shallow or superficial woman on any level," Ceara declared, determined to defend her favorite Dante heroine. "No matter how she continues to feel about Bourne, she definitely wouldn't withdraw her friendship just because of circumstantial evidence."

Hooking his thumbs in the belt loops of his jeans, Vincent leaned against the built-in bookcase and smiled at her. "I knew it would do me good to come and see you."

Fourth of July fireworks went off in her heart, and Ceara smiled back at him. "And here I thought maybe you'd finally decided to let me show you around this place."

He nodded slowly. "Yes. I do believe it's time."

She offered her hand and felt a giddy euphoria when he closed his fingers around hers. It was pure whimsy to think she could lead him anywhere, since he dwarfed her in so many ways. But she liked the feeling of partnership and communication she experienced as she drew him out of the room and across to one of the completed areas.

From the action-and-adventure books, decorated with wildlife prints, a boomerang she had found at an odds-and-ends shop in town, along with a few African masks and several Mayan clay idol reproductions, she took him to World and U.S. History, colorful with national and international flags.

Vincent wandered through several rows of hard and softcover selections before shooting her an impressed look. "Interesting. I see a few things I could use to add to my own library."

Pleased, she led him to the room that held Westerns, then to Science Fiction and Horror, finally ending at the back of the house in what Boone said had been a sun room. Here was where she had moved the biographies and other nonfiction and how-to books. One whole wall was louvered windows and the rest was paneled in cedar that had been painted in a warm honey shade. A rattan love seat was set by the window and was surrounded by numerous tropical plants. And, dividing the room, were two concrete benches separated by an arrangement of tall ficus trees to continue the unique and appealing garden effect.

"This is your favorite, isn't it?" Vincent asked, although he seemed to be scanning titles on the numerous shelves.

Pleased he could tell, Ceara smiled. "Yes. This and the poetry anthology room because of its English-study style. You know me too well."

"Well enough to have always equated you with sunlight. Even your name sounds like the whisper the air makes when it carries the first rays of dawn."

It was one of the loveliest things he had said to her in ages, and as he continued strolling, it took her a moment to realize she was lagging behind. Giving herself a mental shake, she quickly followed.

At the last aisle he stopped by a biography of Henry David Thoreau. His expression was thoughtful as he ran his index finger down its barely creased spine. "I'm beginning to understand why you wanted to embark on this venture."

"Are you?" she asked, acutely aware of her heartbeat echoing in her throat.

"You're going to try to find loving homes for all of these the way a Good Samaritan tries to place an abandoned mongrel or kitten. It's even reflected in that framed quote by Robert Louis Stevenson you have in the entry hall. 'Go, little book, and wish to all, flowers in the garden, meat in the hall...'" He turned to her and his eyes warmed with tenderness. "You want all of these to be happy just as you want everyone around you to be happy."

"You seemed to think that was naive and idealistic before."

"I was being—as your not-so-dear friend Matthew would put it—a boor and selfish. What you are is enviably optimistic, and it's that very quality that draws people to you. Why else is it impossible for me to stay away from you for any length of time?" he added, lifting her hand and directing the rosebud to tilt her chin upward. "Despite knowing I've upset you more than made you smile these days."

"We've both been through a great deal these past months, but I have to admit, as angry and hurt as I have been with your and Dad's machinations, I would have been more upset if you'd done as I'd asked and stayed away."

Vincent moved closer. Reaching up as if to stroke her cheek, he hesitated and instead cupped the back of her head. "Do you mean it?" he asked gruffly, staring into her eyes.

"Yes."

She knew full well what such honesty would yield. Already desire was creating tension in the bold features of his face. He was going to kiss her, and not in anger or frustration as he had before, or as a man claiming what he thought was rightfully his, but with the slow thoroughness of two people sharing what words might bruise.

As their breaths merged and he brushed his lips across hers, Ceara gripped her rose tighter and felt the bite of a thorn. It was no less poignant than the yearning that gripped her heart. Vincent at any given time was compelling and unforgettable; but when gentle, this great, powerful man made her eyes tear and her body melt. Wanting, aching for more, she leaned closer ready, eager to accept whatever he was willing to offer.

The fingers cupping her head shifted and caressed the short locks of her hair before intensifying their pressure to draw her nearer. His mouth, at first as gentle as a phantom breeze, grew more searching. When he slanted his head and fully covered her mouth, Ceara never hesitated in parting her lips to him and met the bold thrust of his tongue.

She heard a sigh before realizing it came from her. She felt the shudder of his powerful body before understanding she was the one striving for even greater contact and pressing against him. And then his arms came fully around her, securing her to him like a vise until from mouth to thigh they could feel each other's heartbeat.

Ceara had dreamed of this kind of fierce tenderness for years only to discover she had underestimated the beauty of its power. Her heart swelled, filled and overflowed with emotions; her body grew hot, weak and achy; and her soul...she moaned softly as her soul sprouted wings and took flight.

The kiss went on and on until Vincent abruptly tore his mouth from hers. "Tell me to stop," he demanded thickly.

"No. I won't help you break my heart ever again."

With a muffled oath he pressed her head into his shoulder. "God," he groaned, burying his face against her hair. "I want you. How I want you."

She smiled, keeping her eyes shut while she enjoyed the heat and trembling in his body. "Tell me how much...or better yet..." Shifting, she tilted back her head to meet his impassioned gaze, took his hand and placed it over her breast.

Despite the thickness of her sweater she knew he could feel her body's instant reaction to his touch, her nipple bead with desire, just as he could feel her hand trembling with nervousness. But she wasn't embarrassed. There had been men who had tried to get her to respond to them; she had been no more able to do so than she could close her eyes without seeing this man's image in her mind's eye. No matter what else happened he needed to understand that.

Vincent's caress was as worshipful, as careful and considerate as he was strong. His big hand easily engulfed her, but he took a small eternity to memorize her shape. Then, abruptly, he pressed his mouth against the side of her neck. "It's too much and not enough. Madness."

"A wonderful madness," she breathed, arching her neck to give him better access.

"I want to see you. In my dreams you're exquisite."

"Only in your dreams?" she challenged softly, aware of being strangely calm.

He uttered another groan. "Dreams, fantasies—they're the perpetual state of my existence now. You fill my nights and I can't sleep, my days and I can't work."

"Do you think it's been any easier for me?"

"I don't allow myself to think about it. I only know that no matter how hard I fight I can't stop coming to get a glimpse of you, hear your voice, pray that you'll let me touch you."

Before Ceara could offer her own viewpoint he claimed her mouth again and led them both on a delirious race toward mindlessness. All she could do was slip her arms around his neck and hold on, because she knew if she tried to stand on her own legs, she would drop at his feet. But just when she was ready to plead or promise him anything, he spun her around so that her back came flush against his chest. He kept her there by wrapping his arms around her.

"No more."

"Vincent—" she gulped for air "—it's all right."

"Don't you *understand?*" Another harsh word erupted from him like a lion's growl. "A few more moments and I'd have been wild enough to lower you onto that flimsy couch." He dragged in a deep breath and stroked his cheek against her hair, gaining control somewhat as he did so. "I have to get out of here."

She leaned into his caress. "Stay. Have lunch with me."

"I can't."

"You haven't seen the upstairs yet." Her thoughts conjured a scene where they were lying on her rose eyelet bedspread while the muted afternoon sun filtered in through the sheer draperies, warming their entwined bodies.

"*I can't.*"

There was regret in his voice, but Ceara was more mindful of the discipline underscoring it. He hadn't forgotten his horrible promise, she warned herself, nor everything else that had been keeping them apart all these years. She broke free and faced him.

"You mean you won't," she said dully. She was tempted to thrust his rose back at him, except that the mere idea of losing it, too, left her feeling physically ill. "You're not the only one who can't continue to go on like this, Vincent."

"If you want to be with me, come spend Thanksgiving at the house. I'm letting Townsend make a fuss. He's planning goose with all the trimmings. Afterward we'll stroll around the grounds. There's a small waterfall I've been wanting to show you forever and—what's wrong?"

She wanted to cry. "It's impossible."

He stiffened, but his hands were gentle as he grasped her shoulders and searched her face. "What do you mean? Why?"

"I'm committed to help serve lunch at the local senior citizen center. It's a chamber-of-commerce-sponsored event, and since I'm one of the new business

owners in the area, I thought . . . no. It's the residents at
the home, Vincent. They're so lonely. I was there a few
days ago to see if they'd like some books, and it broke
my heart to see how eager they were to exchange a few
words with someone from the outside.''

"I see." His tone was understanding, but his expression mirrored deep disappointment. "Naturally, if
you've given your word.''

The kitchen door opened and slammed. "Yoo-hoo!
Ceara, dear, where are you?''

Ceara could have groaned. What timing! "That's
Miss Honeycutt from the inn next door,'' she whispered to Vincent. "She's here to pick up a tablecloth
Naomi had hand-stitched. Boone said she's had her eye
on it forever. I'll only be a minute. Please don't leave.''

Thomasina Honeycutt, however, was in the mood to
chat. Bubbling with her usual enthusiasm and full of
tidbits of gossip, she foiled every attempt Ceara made
to coerce her discreetly to take her package from the
kitchen table and go.

"Miss Honeycutt,'' she said at last, not really caring
if she did sound anxious, "don't you have a lunch
crowd to deal with?''

"Oh, my word!'' The elderly woman pressed a hand
to the brooch at the throat of her high-collared blouse.
"I almost forgot. Lulu said to be sure and borrow that
English cookbook you have. She wants to make scones
or something for this afternoon's tea. I declare, every
time she borrows it I tell her, 'Lucille Louise, now you
remember to write down the recipe this time,' but she
never does.''

Entirely confused, Ceara glanced around the kitchen.
"English cookbook? I'm afraid I don't know . . .''

"Not in here, child. It's with the other cookbooks and things," she said, waving her hand toward the rest of the house.

That had Ceara's heart plummeting. "You mean one of the store books? Wait, Mrs. Honeycutt, if you'll tell me the title, I'll get it for you."

"No need, dear." The woman, upswept Gibson-girl hairdo and all, disappeared around the corner. "I know exactly where it is," she called back.

She went straight into the converted sun room, and Ceara followed, tempted to lasso the woman and tie her to a chair. She was a sweet person—well, entertaining—most of the time. But this wasn't one of those times. Nor was this a lending library, neighbor or not. If it got around that she was making exceptions for one person, where would it end? But most important, Thomasina was an avid gossiper, and if she spotted Vincent and recognized him from his few publicity pictures or started asking awkward questions, it could undo everything they had achieved.

Only he wasn't where she had left him.

"Dear? What have you done with the cookbooks? These are all about repairing automobiles and dripping drains."

"I've switched things around, Miss Honeycutt. They're in the next aisle, but if you'll just tell me—"

"No problem. I can spot it by its binder." Thomasina's ankle-length gabardine skirt rustled as she sped by. "Let's see, it should be . . . no, maybe it's by the books from . . . ah, I remember now. It's right over . . ."

Row after row Ceara followed the whirlwind who didn't seem to know one was supposed to slow down once reaching her age. At each aisle she braced herself, expecting to see Miss Honeycutt's eyes brighten with curiosity and Vincent looking like a man facing a hanging judge. But it didn't happen.

Had he left? Without saying goodbye? Hurt, but swallowing her disappointment, Ceara got a footstool to reach the cookbook Thomasina had spotted on the top shelf. Then she escorted her out.

Tears were blinding her eyes when she walked back down the hall toward the front of the store. It made her all the more ill-prepared when she was grabbed by the waist and pulled into a side room. Spun around before she could catch her breath, she found herself face-to-face with Vincent.

"All right, how about a late dinner?" he suggested, his eyes almost boyish with hope.

"What? Oh!" she gasped, instantly understanding. "Yes! Yes," she cried, wrapping her arms around his neck.

Chapter Nine

*O*ne *of the terrace doors opened and a woman slipped out, quietly closing it behind her. Bourne's whole being went still. Even in the moonlight, even after three years, he recognized her.*

She walked to the edge of the promenade, her step the same smooth glide that had caught his eye the first time he saw her. As she placed her hands flat on the stone wall, she lifted her face to the night. Desire came as it had then, yet stronger, because for three years he'd lived with the memory of what it felt like to touch her, taste her, love her.

God, she'd grown more beautiful. Punishment for his stupidity. He should never have sent her away. She belonged to him. They belonged together. It had taken pushing her away to realize that. And now . . .

He didn't move, but as if she felt his presence, she spun to face him. Cast in shadows, he knew she couldn't identify his dark form; he saw it as fear froze her and widened her eyes.

"Who are you?" she demanded.

"Who do you want me to be?"

For a moment, clutching her silvery-white wrap across her breasts, he saw her stiffen, then waver like a reed in the wind. Slowly she mouthed his name. "Bourne," she said again, this time flying to him.

He caught her, crushed her close and kissed her, then kissed her again like a man starved for air and hope and life. As he was. As he was.

"Ceara—"

Vincent stared at the name that appeared in amber on his computer screen and, groaning, deleted it. The words were pouring from him like water bubbling up from an underground source, seemingly endless, and he was reaching a pivotal part of the story, a part where he needed to be at his sharpest; but for the past half hour he hadn't been able to keep from typing in Ceara's name instead of Anna's.

She was late. He checked his watch again and saw that it was past five and getting dark. She had said she would be here ages ago. Had something gone wrong? Was she hurt? Had she changed her mind? One nightmarish scenario after another had been filling his head, and the only remedy had been to let Bourne Rampal play out his frustrations and dreams.

He slumped back in his chair and eyed the television screen on his security monitor. The only living creature to wander near those wrought-iron gates in hours had been a squirrel in search of acorns. The way things were going, he thought darkly, Townsend would be offering the scavenger their overroasted goose.

Vincent pressed the intercom button to the kitchen. "Is everything in order?" he demanded of his employee.

"Almost, sir."

"'Almost?' You were to be ready at five!"

"I thought it best to allow for delays and a cocktail."

It made admirable sense, but he was in no mood to be so generous. He wanted Ceara here, where he could look at her, touch her and know all was right with the world.

Suddenly a movement brought his attention back to the screen. His heart began to thrum. Good Lord, he thought, staring at the low-slung car pulling up to the gates. Was that matchbox what she was driving these days?

"Townsend, she's here!"

He had his computer shut off, his suede blazer on and was outside before she arrived at the front door. Descending the three wide stairs, he extended a hand as she stepped from her car.

"I'm sorry I'm late."

"All that matters is you're here. How are you? How did everything go?"

"Oh, Vincent, it was so rewarding . . . but exhausting. I need five minutes to catch my breath, or I might fall face first into my dinner plate. I only took ten minutes to run to the house and change clothes."

"And you look lovely." She did, he thought, tenderness and desire churning within him. Beneath a cashmere shawl she was wearing the outfit he had purchased for her after her accident; he couldn't have been more pleased or grateful than if she had sent him an engraved message of her feelings toward him.

Ceara . . . happiness—the words were synonymous. What was more, she was beginning to convince him that he deserved to feel this way. There was no way to be certain he had paid for his past, but he was accepting that it was time to forgive himself if he truly wanted to reach for the preciousness within his grasp.

He led her inside where Townsend greeted them and suggested a few moments in the living room. Wise, Townsend, Vincent thought, directing Ceara there. A fire crackled cheerfully in the fireplace; several bouquets of autumn flowers were artfully scattered around the room and potpourri scented the air with hints of vanilla, cinnamon and orange. On a side table was a silver bowl with mulled cider. When Ceara enthusiastically accepted Townsend's offer of some, Vincent swallowed his previous cynicism and agreed to try a cupful himself.

When they were once again alone, Ceara slipped gracefully into one of the armchairs nearest the fire and sighed with contentment. Vincent thought he would be content to spend the rest of the evening just watching the play of firelight in her hair, eyes and skin.

"Tell me about your day," she coaxed.

"Without you it was long," he admitted. "So I worked. Hard."

"And did it pay off?" she asked, her eyes glowing.

"Thanks to your input, yes. The book's finally coming along. It's . . . different for me, but I like it."

"I'm glad. Then change isn't as bad as you thought?"

"Well . . . my readers might end up arguing with you, but I'm intrigued with the evolving possibilities, yes."

It seemed only seconds before Townsend entered discreetly and asked them if they were ready to move to the dining room. Because Ceara sprang from her chair announcing she was famished, Vincent repressed his impulse to give them another few minutes. And whatever other frustrations he had felt before, he was grateful for the expression on Ceara's face when she saw their table resplendent with chrysanthemums, fruit and branches of evergreens interspersed with candles.

But as glowing as her eyes were before, after the several-course meal, she was radiant. Leaning back in her chair, swearing she couldn't eat another bite of Townsend's homemade cheesecake with its fresh raspberry sauce, she declared, "I'm ready for my walk."

"I'm feeling rather like that plump goose looked myself," Vincent said, hoping this didn't mean she was ready to leave.

"No, I'm serious. Let's do it."

Realizing her remark was meant to be taken literally, he arched an eyebrow. "It's completely dark out there."

"Maybe, but you promised me a waterfall."

"Which is several acres off in the woods through wooded and rocky terrain." He leaned over, glad for the excuse to inspect her small feet encased in soft suede pumps. "I don't think you're dressed for that sort of expedition."

"Technicalities," she said, wagging a finger at him. "I brought along jogging shoes and a jacket. Do you think Townsend can equip us with flashlights?"

Townsend could and did. Once on their way, Vincent made a mental note to thank him later for managing to keep a straight face.

For his part he felt slightly foolish. When he first thought of bringing Ceara to his favorite spot, his intentions were for her to see it in the way he saw her— radiant with sunlight, an endless source of silver and gold reemerging in a crystalline clear pool...a pool giving life. He knew she would adore seeing the bounty of quick-witted fish playing in innocent harmony. Now, he thought glumly, they would be lucky not to fall in themselves.

"Look! We have a moon," Ceara whispered, pointing with her flashlight and hugging his arm tighter as they walked across the leaf-scattered back lawn. "Isn't it romantic, Vincent?"

His heart swelled with love and he smiled, enchanted that she could find magic in this dark, damp cold. He simply saw atmosphere, and a dismal kind at that. "I suppose if it started snowing you'd think you were in heaven?"

"Snow...it must be beautiful here then. With the moon it would look like a dreamworld."

"Haven't you ever been afraid of the dark? The unknown?"

"Of course. But never when you're with me."

Vincent hadn't believed she could say anything to make him feel invincible, but miraculously she had. No longer was he a witness to the night's magic, but a participant. Caught up in the aura, he led her faultlessly to the falls and almost believed it was his heart's whisper to the heavens that opened a pocket of trees to the sky so moonbeams could turn the cascading water into quicksilver. And when Ceara caught her breath and pointed out a deer downstream that had eyed them without fear and contentedly bent to quench its thirst, he understood they were caught up in something momentous. It was impossible to live through this moment, he thought, and not believe more, *anything* was possible.

"Do you feel it, Vincent?" Ceara laid a hand on his chest and gazed up at him. "I've never known a more perfect moment."

Stars shimmered in her lovely eyes. Her lips were more tempting than the succulent berries that had reddened them at dinner. Moonlight turned her flawless skin to alabaster. Gazing down at the center of his universe, Vincent couldn't have agreed more, and followed a need more necessary than breathing. "Perfect," he murmured, lowering his mouth to hers.

He felt like a weary and frozen traveler being invited to come closer to a vibrant campfire. When she slid the hand she was resting against his chest up around his nape to draw him closer, he whispered, "Ceara," against her lips and gratefully took what she so sweetly offered.

Then there was only their merging, the sensual, breathtaking reaching and blending of essences. As desire swelled and passion bloomed, Vincent felt Ceara move completely into his arms. With a low growl of approval, joy and passion he lifted her completely against him. She weighed less than a dream, but she was everything he wanted and he showed her again and again until they were both trembling with unfulfilled passion.

"I've never wanted like this," he whispered between raining kisses over her face, her neck, anywhere he could reach. "Do you understand? Never."

"I want you, too. We belong together, Vincent," she murmured, stroking his hair back from his brow. "We always have."

Yes, he knew it. And he knew walls were crumbling between them, new bonds were forming, strengthening. But he couldn't conquer one last worry. If he rushed things, a small voice warned, made love to her and took what he craved most, he wouldn't be able to let her go again. Did he have a right without giving her the assurance the old Vincent Dante was gone forever?

"Do you trust me, Ceara?"

She searched his face. Worry clouded her eyes, but he could see her force it away and nod bravely.

"Then give things, *us* a little more time. Tonight is a beginning. Let's savor it."

"If that's what you want," she whispered.

"No, my precious. What I want is to make love with you until the sun rises and we fall asleep in each other's arms. But I couldn't bear to disappoint you afterward and so . . . it's what I need."

It's what I need.

"Ceara, this is the most exciting thing that's ever happened to me."

Ceara forced herself out of her private brooding and smiled at Nydia Berenson's gushed declaration. This was her big night, she reminded herself, placing her empty tray on the clearest portion of the kitchen's central counter that she could find. "What about Colin and the children?" she teased gently.

"Well, I mean *after* my marriage and my babies," Nydia replied. "Do you know every author I've introduced myself to tonight has been so . . . so . . ."

"Normal?"

"Exactly. They're like real people." Nydia's dark eyes went wide, her eyelashes disappearing beneath her raven bangs. The heavy silver bracelets on each of her wrists caught the overhead fluorescent lights and flashed as brightly as her smile as she deftly refilled her own tray with hors d'oeuvres.

"They're normal all right," Boone muttered, opening another can of olives. "If there's a free meal to be had, they eat like horses."

Ceara quickly visualized what she wanted for her own tray. "It's your own fault for being such a marvelous cook. Your crab spread is the hit of the party. If you ever decide to go into catering, you could book any number of events in the Mapleton area alone. The mayor's especially taken with the filling in those marinated mushroom caps."

"Hmph...call that a compliment? I hear the man had a healthy appetite at his own mother's funeral reception. How long before these people start going home, anyway?"

Ceara exchanged an amused grin with Nydia. "It's barely after eight. You know the invitations read seventhirty to nine-thirty."

"The thing worrying me is we'd anticipated some people would just pop in and leave," Nydia interjected. "So far everyone's staying. If any more guests arrive, I don't know where we're going to put them. By the way, has anyone seen Mr. Pritchard lately?"

Ceara nodded. "He's tending the bar in the history room and carrying on a lively political debate with my former boss."

"Pritchard?" Boone sniffed. "He didn't strike me as having enough blood in him to get excited about anything."

Although Ceara silently admitted she had wondered the same thing during the job interview with the pale, broomstick of a man, she had no such hesitation about defending him now. "Mr. Pritchard prides himself on exercising cerebral strength rather than physical brawn, and from what I've discovered he's quite a heavy-weight.''

"Isn't it nice he and Mr. Townsend have become friends?" Nydia asked, arranging a few sprigs of pars-ley around her platter. "They've been meeting for weekly chess matches. And how kind of Mr. Townsend to have made you his special rum cake for tonight."

Yes, Ceara thought, he was wonderful. She only wished she could be as sure of his employer. Where *was* Vincent? she wondered, experiencing another pang of worry.

She had invited him to tonight's event. It had meant so much to share this with him, especially when things seemed to be going so well between them since Thanks-giving. Of course, with his book deadline and her preparations their moments together had been fewer than she would have liked, but he *had* accepted her in-vitation.

Reluctantly.

Panic rose like a geyser. What if he decided not to come? No, she couldn't bear to let herself think such a thing. It would mean she had been foolish in believing they had overcome their previous problems and that would devastate her. She had a party to hostess.

"Ceara?"

"Sorry?"

"I said it was nice of Mr. Townsend to make you that cake."

"Wasn't it?" It was easier to smile when she had someone else's thoughtfulness to focus on. "He told me the recipe was his mother's. Have you had a chance to taste any?"

"Only as I was placing it on the platter. That raisin sauce alone could knock out someone. What's the secret?"

"Jamaica rum."

"Don't know why you had to put it by them cackling women," Boone complained. "Most of them's got hips that don't need any more padding."

"I thought you said you liked your women with a little meat on their bones?" Nydia teased.

Boone glared back at her defiantly. "Less talk and more work, missy."

She expelled a playful groan and lifted her tray. "Aye-aye, Captain Bligh. I'm out of here."

Ceara watched her new employee cautiously ease her petite body out through the swinging door. The momentary buzz of voices grew into a medium roar and then quieted again. She would have to remember to tell Nydia again how much she liked her black-and-silver satin outfit.

She had high hopes for Nydia. The young mother, only a few years older than Ceara herself, had put her own career aspirations on hold while she had started a family and supported her husband's budding law career. Now that Colin had been elected as the youngest district attorney in county history and both children were in school, Nydia was finally able to make use of her business degree and her love of books to learn this angle of the retail business. Although it was too early to plan, Ceara could see Nydia taking over the management of the store for her, or becoming a full partner if that was something she found appealing.

"Good Lord, it's a blizzard out there."

Lost in her own thoughts, it took Ceara a moment to realize Boone had gone outside to retrieve another air sealed container of shrimp on ice for the center of her tray. They had been grateful to be able to use the cold weather in addition to their cramped refrigerator, but a snowfall was something else.

"The ground's covered and it doesn't look like it's going to end anytime soon," Boone concluded.

Ceara hurried to the back door to take a peek, worried for her local guests who would be driving home tonight. Sure enough the porch light illuminated a cascade of large, fluffy snowflakes falling to an already white-blanketed earth. "I suppose things could have been worse. It could have started before anyone got here. Thank goodness the New York group were able to book rooms next door, but I may tell Nydia to leave sooner."

After suggesting to Boone to bring in the champagne from outside and store what he could in the refrigerator when space allowed, she followed Nydia to deliver her tray to the front buffet table.

"Ceara, dear, I was wondering where you'd disappeared to."

She allowed herself to be drawn into the doorway of the history room and accepted a kiss on the cheek from a scarlet-taloned Murella Van Cleefe, wife of the president of the chamber of commerce.

"Lovely event, darling. I've just been telling Sylvia that this is exactly what the town needed to get it out of its too-comfortable little rut. Having your celebrity friends and the New York people visiting periodically will put Mapleton on the map the way it was when my grandfather was mayor. Didn't I say that, Sylvia? Now things were run right then. Why only yesterday..."

After about thirty seconds, Ceara met banker Sylvia Bakersfeld's droll wink and ducked her head to keep a straight face. Everyone knew, within moments of meeting Murella, that the woman loved to hear herself talk.

"Stop spouting such nonsense," Sylvia drawled in a voice lower than any man's within hearing distance. "Your grandfather was a pirate who filled his pockets well before he worried about the cultural enlightenment of this town, and everyone knows it."

"That's not true!" Wounded, Murella looked from her friend to Ceara. "It's not. Just because he was successful people are envious. At any rate, I was only complimenting Ceara."

"Thank you. It means a great deal to me that you approve," Ceara said, taking advantage of the opportunity to extricate herself. She took a side step down the hall. "But I really must get this food up front. Enjoy yourselves, ladies."

She actually made it to the front room before she was roadblocked again. This time her nemesis was the mayor.

"Why, thank you, Ceara, don't mind if I do." Winston James plucked up another stuffed mushroom, but instead of popping it into his mouth as she expected, he leaned toward her and whispered conspiratorially, "Why didn't you tell me you'd managed to pull off the coup of the century? More important, how'd you do it?"

"I'm afraid I don't understand."

"*Him.*" With a discreet tilt of his balding head he indicated the far side of the room. "How'd you convince our resident icon to grace us with his presence? I've been trying to get him to be a grand marshal at our July Fourth parade, a keynote speaker at the annual Mapleton Auxiliary Roast—you name it. But he's always turned me down."

Ceara stopped hearing the mayor the moment she
ollowed his nod and located the object of his interest.
t that very moment Vincent looked up and met her
tunned gaze.

He stood in the darkest corner of the room, looking
minent and compelling in his black dinner suit, and
nything but enthralled with having gotten himself into
 position where people were jockeying to get closer to
im. He was handing a woman back her book and pen
nd, like Ceara, had momentarily frozen when their
azes locked.

She was so relieved and thrilled to see him that she
ouldn't find the words to answer the mayor. All she
ould think was that he hadn't let her down. More im-
ortant, he had overcome his own aversion to public-
y. It could mean only one thing—anything was
ossible for them.

"You weren't sure he'd show, either?"

"Well, I . . ." She had thought it best not to tell any-
ne because she had been afraid Vincent might change
is mind at the last minute. But how did she explain that
 the mayor? she wondered, tearing her gaze from
'incent's and looking blankly at Winston James.

He grimaced and, gulping down his snack, stopped
ne of the three college boys Ceara had hired to serve
hampagne. "Here, I'll trade you," he said, scooping
he last two glasses of wine from the young man's tray
ith one hand and awarding him Ceara's tray of hors
'oeuvres with the other. "You look like you need
iis," he explained, presenting her with one of the
lasses.

"Actually, you couldn't be more wrong." But Ceara
ccepted the glass, anyway. She had a feeling who might
eed it.

"When you go over and welcome him," Winston wheedled, "I'd like an introduction."

"It won't help you."

"Oh, I don't know," Winston said, glancing from her to Vincent and back again. "I have a feeling I'd fare a lot better with you by my side than without you."

Aware that if she wasn't careful it would only be a matter of time before everyone else in the room picked up on the chemistry between them, Ceara wondered if Vincent would mind. But when as before their gazes connected and clung, it ceased to matter. *Dear heaven, he's magnificent,* she thought, walking toward him.

Dear heaven, she's lovely, Vincent thought, willing her to come to him with all his being. He needed her near; nothing else would keep terror at bay. If he could just look at her and draw in her unique, springlike scent, he could intoxicate himself into coping with this fiasco. She was wearing a burgundy full-length gown made of something soft and clingy, but cut with the utmost taste high at the throat and long at the sleeve. Gold earrings in a wing design were the only jewelry she wore—unless one counted her eyes, which glowed like gems. The emotions he read in their depths had his blood pounding even faster in his veins.

"Mr. Dante? My book, please?"

Vincent forced himself to focus on the woman beside him and saw blue-permed hair and glasses thick enough to make her a traffic hazard even if she did wear them while driving. She offered a sweet smile that once again prompted him to wonder about the people who read his work. He had no understanding of them whatsoever, or their desire to meet him and have something with his signature on it. He wrote for himself, stories

hat intrigued him. Granted, he was grateful numbers
f people seemed to share his taste. But what made
hem think *he* was as interesting as his work?

"Thank you," he murmured. He handed book and
en back to her, belatedly glancing at the jacket of the
olume he had signed. It was Ceara's favorite. But he
ad only a second to understand and appreciate that
efore another book was thrust at him. "Your name?"
e asked mechanically.

"Mr. Dante, I want you to know I normally buy all
f your books in hardcover. This one's only paperback
ecause by the time I heard someone whisper you were
ere everyone had beaten me to the stack of your new
ardcover release."

"Thank you. Your name?"

The woman told him, and then didn't stop talking
ven when he handed her book back to her. Ignoring the
hree that were shoved at him once the woman reluc-
antly relinquished her place, he saw Ceara being drawn
n the opposite direction by a distinguished gray-haired
1an. Dread and jealousy blazed within him, and he
vanted to burst through the crowd and smash his fist
nto the man's tanned, photogenic face.

He forced himself to sign a few more books before he
ooked for her again. Rather than making any prog-
2ss, she had been drawn deeper into the crowd.

"You look like a Scotch man to me."

Vincent focused on the tumbler with the amber liq-
.id and ice and accepted it as soon as he passed over
1other book. He took a deep swallow and only then
onsidered his rescuer. It was the stocky, dimple-faced
1an who had tried to bring Ceara to him. "Thank
ou . . ."

"Winston James."

The name meant nothing to him. "Agent? Editor?"

"Mayor. And actually I lied. Ceara asked me to get you this."

"I owe you, Mr. Mayor," Vincent drawled, saluting him with his glass before taking another drink.

The man's face lit up and a wide grin connected dimple to dimple. "Well, now...I certainly hope you mean that."

"Ceara? We need you in the back," Nydia whispered near her ear. "Emergency."

Now what? Ceara thought, shooting a worried glance toward Vincent. The crowd around him hadn't diminished, and she knew if she could slip her hand beneath his jacket, she would find his back soaking wet. If only she could tell him how proud and grateful she was that he had ventured this big step.

"*Ceara.*"

"Yes, right away." Her own needs and wants would have to wait. With a sigh she followed Nydia.

The problem turned out to be a dropped platter by one of the young men and Boone's subsequent tantrum. Nothing a cool head couldn't handle. Ceara pacified Boone, soothed the chagrined young man and helped Nydia get another platter ready.

As soon as things were once again calm in the kitchen, she headed back toward the front. She was stopped midway by Winston.

"He's gone."

"No!"

"Apparently the Scotch I poured him didn't quite do the trick. It happened after a fan introduced himself—actually it was someone who'd been a former student of

Dante's father—that he excused himself, saying he'd left his cigarettes in his car. He hasn't come back.''

"Probably because there were no cigarettes in his car,'' Ceara murmured.

"Pardon?''

Feeling a claustrophobia and nausea that must be only a shadow of what Vincent was experiencing, Ceara shook her head. "I'm sorry. I have to—'' She headed back toward the kitchen.

Boone took one look at her face, dropped the pan he was scrubbing into the sink and began wiping his hands in his apron. "What now?''

"I have to leave.''

"You've got a house full of people. The roads are treacherous. Is any of that making an impression on you?''

She shook her head. "Something's happened. Someone I care about very much needs me. Oh, God...'' She pressed her palms to her temples, trying to convince herself it was the sane thing to do. Her heart said it was, but then when had *it* ever been more than trouble?

"This is important?''

"Yes.'' She met his clear, wise eyes. "*Yes.*''

"Then grab your coat and get a move on. I'll tell Nydia and Pritchard. Between us we'll manage.''

"But I wanted Nydia to leave herself.''

"Her husband called. He's got a neighbor sitting with the young ones and he's on his way to get her. Heck, it's nearly time to close shop, anyway, and I'd like to be the one to chase everyone out of here. I'm only fooling,'' he said when she shot him a horrified look. "Now get. Here.'' He led her to the back door and took her coat off the rack, holding it up for her to slip on.

On the back porch in ankle-deep snow with heavy flakes already weighing down her lashes, Ceara glanced back at the old man. ''I owe you an explanation,'' she told him.

''A call letting me know you're all right will do fine.''

''As soon as I can.'' With tears of gratitude burning in her eyes Ceara quickly kissed his cheek. Then, hoisting her skirt with one hand and clinging to the railing with the other, she navigated through the snow in her high heels.

Chapter Ten

When Ceara chose her red sports car, she told herself it was a symbol of independence, the hallmark of a new path in her life. She thought she had a right to be impulsive. But as she inched her way through town, she felt her tires slip again and again on the snow and wished she had listened to her father's lectures about all the benefits of bigger, heavier models. At least traffic was nonexistent, she thought, clutching the steering wheel.

Now that she was on her way all the doubts about leaving her party came back to haunt her. People were going to ask questions. She hadn't told Boone what to tell them. Nydia and Mr. Pritchard would be concerned, not to mention feel left out or even abandoned. And yet, despite all the doubts, she knew none of it mattered compared to this.

Vincent was probably torturing himself, calling himself a failure and a few less polite things. He also wouldn't be thrilled when he learned that once again she could see through his shield of confidence and aloofness and understood his pain. But if he thought she was going to keep standing by and letting him deal with his problems alone, he was wrong. He had *tried* to attend her party; that was one giant step she wouldn't let him back away from.

She turned on her windshield wipers to the maximum speed. Once the car began to warm, she stamped one foot and then the other to knock off the rest of the snow and warm her frozen toes.

Headlights appeared up ahead; a vehicle was coming around the bend. Automatically Ceara hit the brakes. *Wrong,* her subconscious screamed, even as she felt the car's rear wheels slide to the right and the front pair to the left. She had no time to think about the one lesson she'd had regarding driving in snow and dealing with skids. She was veering across the now-invisible line in the road. The oncoming vehicle would hit her if she didn't do something fast.

Anything was better than a head-on collision, Ceara decided, and let the car continue its course. She changed her mind the instant she went off the road and the sports car began bucking like a rodeo bull.

Gratefully the ride was brief. Except for one horrifying second when she thought she was going to flip over completely, the car came to an abrupt nose-down halt in a ditch.

When Vincent saw the red sports car jerk to a stop at a teetering angle, he uttered an oath of relief. For a moment he had believed it was Ceara, but that was impossible. She was so wrapped up in celebration party obligations, they hadn't been able to say hello to each other.

Carefully easing his four-wheel-drive vehicle to the shoulder of the road, he put on the warning flashers and reached for his flashlight. The sports car didn't look damaged, but whoever had been driving would be damn lucky if they weren't bruised or cut.

Turning up the collar of his coat, he set off to offer his assistance. He was in no mood to play Good Samaritan; whoever the driver was, he deserved to spend some time out here to ponder his foolhardiness. As for himself, he had his own agenda and he needed to take care of it before anyone noticed his absence.

Rounding the driver's side, he directed the beam of his flashlight to the door swinging open. Through the blur of falling snow he spotted a pair of shapely legs in dainty high heels emerging and disappearing into a drift of snow. He shivered at the mere thought of how cold it must feel. Then the driver squirmed out of the car and empathy turned to shock.

Ceara?

He covered the last few yards in a lunge. She barely had time to gasp against the cold, or recognize it was he who had come to her aid. He swept her off her feet and into his arms.

"What are you . . . oh!"

"I'm going to hire you a chauffeur," he muttered, crushing his mouth to hers as punishment for scaring the life out of him . . . and to prove to himself that she was safe. When his chest began to burn with the need for oxygen, he buried his face against her neck and shuddered. "Oh, God."

She touched his cheek. "I'm all right, Vincent. Truly."

Her trembling, icy fingers contradicted the claim, but she would be better soon. He would see to it.

Setting her on the trunk, he muttered, "Stay put," and leaned inside her car. He snatched out her keys and searched for her purse. "Where's your bag?" he called, unable to locate it.

"I suppose I forgot it," she admitted, ducking deeper into her coat to escape the intensifying wind.

"Another stroke of genius. You go out on a night like this without any identification?" He expended his temper by slamming the door hard enough for the whole vehicle to shake. When he plucked her off the trunk and close so that they were nose to nose, he was able to be grateful again. "You're lucky I'm not the police with a quota to meet, my love."

He could feel her eyes on him as he fought the wind and carried her to his car. Even after he placed her in the passenger seat and went around to the driver's side, her stare was as intense as a prison searchlight.

The moment he slammed his own door she demanded, "Where were you headed just now?"

"Isn't it obvious?"

She shot him an impressive duplication of his own arched stare. "Your *cigarettes* weren't in your car so you decided to drive all the way home for them? That's quite a nicotine habit you've developed, considering you despise the things almost as much as you do crowds and attracting attention."

He should have known she would find out. "Our mayor talks too much."

"You'd say that about a block of salt."

"Well, at least he's given me an excuse to back out of that ridiculous speech I can't believe I agreed to. It's all your fault, you know," he added, carefully brushing lingering snowflakes from her hair. "If I hadn't been so obsessed with trying to make my way to you, I wouldn't have been so willing to barter my so-called marketability to that publicity hound."

"How far did you get before you decided to come back?" she asked, matching his quiet, lazy tone.

"I turned around about a mile up the road."

"Why?"

"Because I realized I was ready to stop running." It wasn't easy to push the dungeon gates all the way open. After all these years, they were rusty, stubborn. "Why did you come after me?"

Ceara gazed out beyond the streams of melting snowflakes on the windshield. "Because I needed you to know you weren't alone and that you were more important to me than any business ever could be. I came because I love you...and I can't change that. I realized tonight I'll keep coming after you until you crush out the last ounce of that love...because I don't know how to make my heart stop caring."

And he had been worried about their age difference? Once again she was proving to be the stronger, wiser and better of the two of them. Perhaps if he kept a studious vigil for the next thirty or forty years, he might learn to be a worthy match.

Giving in to his need to touch her again, he reached over to draw her onto his lap. "Feel this," he muttered, taking her still-cold hand and drawing it inside his coat and jacket, and against his pounding heart. "This is for you. Because of you. It's been like this from the beginning. It always will be."

"Now I believe you love me," she whispered, splaying her fingers wide to touch as much of him as she could.

He closed his eyes as a shuddering sigh rose from deep within. "Love you? I adore you," he rasped, shifting his hand to frame her face. "You're everything to me. Everything." And to punctuate that he kissed her with all the reverence and devotion radiating from his heart.

Ceara eagerly wrapped her arms around his neck. "Oh, Vincent, *Vincent*." She hugged him tightly. "I was so proud of what you did tonight. So—"

"Kiss me." Reverence gave way to more primal emotions and, as Ceara shifted to get closer to him, Vincent angled his head to lock his mouth more firmly to hers. Their tongues met, tempted and tangled, and soon the heat of passion proved countless times more satisfying than what the car was blowing at them through the vents.

Vincent felt barriers crashing down around him like great mortar walls, and he shuddered, but couldn't stop showing Ceara how deeply he loved her and how desperately he wanted her. Soon his body throbbed with that longing, and it became torture to think how long it would be before he could make her completely his.

"I should be telling you how breathtaking you look tonight," he murmured, running his hand up and down her body the way he had been yearning to.

"So do you."

"I wanted to kill every man there who looked at you."

"And I wanted to evict every woman making calf-eyes at you."

Instead of laughing he grew serious. "Ceara...the past may continue to intrude no matter how hard I try to put it behind me."

"You're thinking about the man who was there tonight, the man who'd been a student of your father's?"

"Yes."

"Does he know everything?"

"I don't think so. He graduated the year before it all happened. But there are numerous others who might show up at any time."

"Let them. It's done, Vincent. Granted, you can't change the past, but anyone who spends any time around you can see how you've strived to become a better person because of the lessons you've learned ... and you have." She offered him a sweet smile. "And never forget I'll always be right beside you whenever you need me."

"I'll need you for the rest of my life," he growled, holding her fast. "Ceara ... marry me."

Although her eyes sparkled with amber stars, she remained as earnest as he. "Be sure, Vincent. I couldn't bear it if you changed your mind."

"I won't and I am. Marry me. I may not be a saint, but no man will ever treasure you more than I do. Say it. Say, 'Yes, Vincent, I'll be your wife.'"

"I'll be your wife, your lover, soul mate and anything else you want me to be. I'll even sell the store if you think it might cause problems for us."

He was taken aback by her willingness to sacrifice so much. "After all the work and time you've invested in it? No, you need an intellectual outlet as much as anyone else. If the store will give you that—" He couldn't finish because she had begun to rain a new torrent of kisses on his face. He had to concentrate to remember what else he wanted to say. "I may ask you to cut your hours once the baby comes," he murmured, slipping his hand to her flat belly. Her dumbfounded expression was precious. "What?" he teased. "You thought I was such an ogre I'd deprive you, *us* of that?"

"I was afraid you'd worry about your age again."

"Twenty years ago I would have pitied any child I helped bring into this world. I was shallow and selfish and nowhere near ready to take on the responsibility of being a father. No, this is right. I may not be the sprinter I was twenty years ago, but I'm much better at everything else." And just imagining her with his son or daughter growing inside her only inspired a new wave of desire. "How long do you think you'd want to wait before . . ."

"Before . . . ?"

"Precisely," he murmured as they interrupted each other with long, increasingly hungry kisses.

Ceara communicated her reply without words, and soon the windows were completely fogged and their sighs were as shallow as they were unsteady. It was only the flare of headlights that brought them back to reality.

With a groan Vincent reluctantly set her back in her seat. As soon as the car was past, he made a U-turn and headed back toward his house, telling her he would call to have her car towed in the morning. "Do you mind?" he added. "I'm not ready to share you with anyone else yet."

Ceara reassured him that she felt the same way. Five minutes later he was pulling up beneath the portico of his house. "Allow me," he said, once again lifting her into his arms. "Those shoes look too treacherous for my peace of mind."

He carried her inside, his footsteps echoing in the dimly lit foyer. But despite the low lights both he and

Ceara spotted the wine decanter placed by the poinsettia arrangement on the center table. Inside was a bottle of vintage champagne and beside it two crystal glasses.

"You were that sure of yourself?" Ceara murmured, her expression bemused.

"Anything but. This must be Townsend's doing. The question is, how did he know?"

"Good instincts?"

She nuzzled his jawline, which prompted him to seek another long kiss until desire was clawing at him. "I want you," he breathed against her lips. "I want to take you upstairs to my bed, undress you, worship you and—very patiently, very permanently—make you mine. Does that frighten you?"

"Vincent, the only thing frightening me is that I might suddenly realize this is all a dream."

His mouth as parched as a desert salt flat, Vincent nodded at the wine and glasses and rasped, "Can you get those?"

She did and he turned toward the stairs. "If it is a dream," he whispered gruffly, "it's one we never have to wake from." And feeling proud and grateful and desperately in love, he started up the steps.

Townsend waited until he heard the upstairs door shut before stepping from the unlit hall. He crossed the foyer and picked up the ice bucket, indulging in a smile as he thought of the changes he had to look forward to. It would be good to have laughter in this house, he thought, and light.

His gaze was drawn into the dark living room, and he decided tomorrow morning over breakfast wouldn't be too soon to broach the subject of a Christmas tree with Miss Ceara.

After double-locking the front door, he turned out the light and returned to his quarters, humming softly under his breath.

*   *   *   *   *

**HE'S MORE THAN
A MAN, HE'S
ONE OF OUR**

EMMETT
Diana Palmer

What a way to start the new year! Not only is Diana Palmer's
EMMETT the first of our new series, FABULOUS FATHERS, but
it's her 10th LONG, TALL TEXANS and her 50th book for
Silhouette!

Emmett Deverell was at the end of his lasso. His three children
had become uncontrollable! The long, tall Texan knew they
needed a mother's influence, and the only female offering was
Melody Cartman. Emmett would rather be tied to a cactus than
deal with that prickly woman. But Melody proved to be softer
than he'd ever imagined....

Don't miss Diana Palmer's EMMETT, available in January.

Fall in love with our FABULOUS FATHERS—and join the
Silhouette Romance family!

R O M A N C E™

OFFICIAL RULES • MILLION DOLLAR MATCH 3 SWEEPSTAKES
NO PURCHASE OR OBLIGATION NECESSARY TO ENTER

To enter, follow the directions published. **ALTERNATE MEANS OF ENTRY:** Hand print y
name and address on a 3" ×5" card and mail to either: Silhouette "Match 3," 3010 Wal
Ave., P.O. Box 1867, Buffalo, NY 14269-1867, or Silhouette "Match 3," P.O. Box 609,
Erie, Ontario L2A 5X3, and we will assign your Sweepstakes numbers. (Limit: one entry
envelope.) For eligibility, entries must be received no later than March 31, 1994. No resp
sibility is assumed for lost, late or misdirected entries.

Upon receipt of entry, Sweepstakes numbers will be assigned. To determine winne
Sweepstakes numbers will be compared against a list of randomly preselected prizewinn
numbers. In the event all prizes are not claimed via the return of prizewinning numbers,
dom drawings will be held from among all other entries received to award unclaimed priz

Prizewinners will be determined no later than May 30, 1994. Selection of winning nu
bers and random drawings are under the supervision of D.L. Blair, Inc., an independent judg
organization, whose decisions are final. One prize to a family or organization. No subst
tion will be made for any prize, except as offered. Taxes and duties on all prizes are the s
responsibility of winners. Winners will be notified by mail. Chances of winning are de
mined by the number of entries distributed and received.

Sweepstakes open to persons 18 years of age or older, except employees and immedi
family members of Torstar Corporation, D.L. Blair, Inc., their affiliates, subsidiaries and
other agencies, entities and persons connected with the use, marketing or conduct of
Sweepstakes. All applicable laws and regulations apply. Sweepstakes offer void where
prohibited by law. Any litigation within the province of Quebec respecting the conduct a
awarding of a prize in this Sweepstakes must be submitted to the Régies des Loteries et Cour
du Quebec. In order to win a prize, residents of Canada will be required to correctly answ
a time-limited arithmetical skill-testing question. Values of all prizes are in U.S. currency.

Winners of major prizes will be obligated to sign and return an affidavit of eligibility a
release of liability within 30 days of notification. In the event of non-compliance within t
time period, prize may be awarded to an alternate winner. Any prize or prize notification
turned as undeliverable will result in the awarding of that prize to an alternate winner. By
ceptance of their prize, winners consent to use of their names, photographs or other likeness
for purposes of advertising, trade and promotion on behalf of Torstar Corporation withe
further compensation, unless prohibited by law.

This Sweepstakes is presented by Torstar Corporation, its subsidiaries and affiliates
conjunction with book, merchandise and/or product offerings. Prizes are as follows: Gra
Prize—$1,000,000 (payable at $33,333.33 a year for 30 years). First through Sixth Priz
may be presented in different creative executions, each with the following approximate v
ues: First Prize—$35,000; Second Prize—$10,000; 2 Third Prizes—$5,000 each; 5 Fou
Prizes—$1,000 each; 10 Fifth Prizes—$250 each; 1,000 Sixth Prizes—$100 each. Pri
winners will have the opportunity of selecting any prize offered for that level. A travel-pr
option, if offered and selected by winner, must be completed within 12 months of select
and is subject to hotel and flight accommodations availability. Torstar Corporation may p
sent this Sweepstakes utilizing names other than Million Dollar Sweepstakes. For a curr
list of all prize options offered within prize levels and all names the Sweepstakes may utili
send a self-addressed, stamped envelope (WA residents need not affix return postage)
Million Dollar Sweepstakes Prize Options/Names, P.O. Box 4710, Blair,[fj NE 68009.

The Extra Bonus Prize will be awarded in a random drawing to be conducted no later th
May 30, 1994 from among all entries received. To qualify, entries must be received by Mai
31, 1994 and comply with published directions. No purchase necessary. For complete rul
send a self-addressed, stamped envelope (WA residents need not affix return postage)
Extra Bonus Prize Rules, P.O. Box 4600, Blair, NE 68009.

For a list of prizewinners (available after July 31, 1994) send a separate, stamped, se
addressed envelope to: Million Dollar Sweepstakes Winners, P.O. Box 4728, Bla
NE 68009.

Silhouette

CHRISTMAS

Stories
1992

Experience the beauty of Yuletide romance with Silhouette
Christmas Stories 1992—a collection of heartwarming stories b[...]
favorite Silhouette authors.

JONI'S MAGIC by Mary Lynn Baxter
HEARTS OF HOPE by Sondra Stanford
THE NIGHT SANTA CLAUS RETURNED by Marie Ferrarrella
BASKET OF LOVE by Jeanne Stephens

Also available this year are three popular early editions of
Silhouette Christmas Stories—1986, 1987 and 1988. Look for
these and you'll be well on your way to a complete collection
of the best in holiday romance.

Plus, as an added bonus, you can receive a FREE keepsake
Christmas ornament. Just collect four proofs of purchase from
any November or December 1992 Harlequin or Silhouette serie[...]
novels, or from any Harlequin or Silhouette Christmas
collection, and receive a beautiful dated brass Christmas
candle ornament.

Mail this certificate along with four (4) proof-of-purchase coupons, plus $1.50 postage a[...]
handling (check or money order—do not send cash), payable to Silhouette Books, to: **In N**
U.S.: P.O. Box 9057, Buffalo, NY 14269-9057; **In Canada:** P.O. Box 622, Fort Erie, Ontar[...]
L2A 5X3.

ONE PROOF OF
PURCHASE

SX92POP

Name: _____

_____

Address: _____

_____

City: _____

State/Province: _____

Zip/Postal Code: _____

093 KAG